S

THRILLS
DANGER
SUSPENSE
MYSTERY

IMPRINT

THE GREAT
MELBOURNE CUP
MYSTERY

Arthur Upfield

Introduced & Edited by
Stuart Mayne

An IMPRINT book
Imprint is a division of ETT Imprint
11 Cove Street, Watsons Bay NSW 2030, Australia.

First published in 1996.

Distributed in Australia by Tower Books.

ISBN 1-875892-56-7

Cover and internal design by Blow-up Pty Ltd, Double Bay.
Printed by Southbank, Fishermans Bend, Victoria.

Contents

Introdustion by Stuart Mayne

1	A Strange Side Bet	*1*
2	'When You Are Ready'	*7*
3	A Sporting Run	*15*
4	'I'll Try It'	*21*
5	In a Hurry	*27*
6	A Man and Three Horses	*35*
7	The Doctor	*42*
8	'Silly Little Fool'	*49*
9	His Chance	*55*
10	The Stranger	*61*
11	Will Do Well	*67*
12	The Letter	*74*
13	The Mysterious Mr Leader	*81*
14	A Good Trainer	*85*
15	'They're Off	*92*
16	Taken For a Ride	*98*
17	The Parade	*105*
18	21 Starters	*109*
19	Met Trouble	*117*
20	Knifed!	*124*
21	Too Old	*130*
22	Very Strange	*138*
23	The Police	*141*
24	Mother Hubbard	*146*
25	'Dented Three Heads'	*150*
26	Poisoned Needle	*156*
27	A Piece of Scalp	*163*
28	In Grave Danger	*169*
29	The Scorpion	*175*
30	The Hooded Man	*181*
31	Aftermath	*186*
	Glossary	*193*

Introduction

The horse racing track has always acted as a lure to the crime author. *The Great Melbourne Cup Mystery* is set during the racing season leading up to and following the running of the Melbourne Cup. Arthur W. Upfield (1882-1964), giant of Australian crime fiction—by virtue of his creation of the part Aboriginal detective, Napoleon Bonaparte—successfully put his pen to the task that inspired the likes of Nat Gould, Agatha Christie, Edgar Wallace and Dick Francis.

Horse racing has always held an important place in Australian culture. Through the early days of colonisation, especially the early days of Melbourne, to the 1930s, horse racing out stripped the popularity of cricket and Australian Rules Football. Even today horse racing is the second most popular spectator sport in Australia, after Australian Rules Football.

The first race meeting at Melbourne was held on 6-7 March 1838. The track for this race started at the present site of the North Melbourne railway station and ended at the foot of Batman's Hill, where Spencer St. railway station now stands.

The next year the same race meeting was held on the ground called 'The Racecourse'. After a name change The Racecourse became Flemington Racecourse, named after a local butcher, Bob Fleming. This racecourse is the present site of the Melbourne Cup, raced on the first Tuesday of November every year.

Many Australians, whether they lived in the country or in the city, have always gambled on a race horse. Indeed, *The Great Melbourne Cup Mystery* begins with a once popular form of race meeting, the country picnic race meeting. Like a country cricket match, the picnic race meeting was less serious than city events. The emphasis of the picnic race was on community togetherness, rather than high stakes betting or valuable cups. When owners try to run their horses 'dead' at these meetings the scam becomes a comic spectacle, rather than a villainous plot.

The business that horse racing became in early Australia offered many opportunities for corruption. Rigged races with horses exceeding their previous form by way of a double, or ring in; promising horses being 'nobbled' and fixing the jockey's weights have all been popular forms of corruption in horse racing. By no means have these practices been isolated to Australia, but in this country the verve and popularity of the sport of horse racing has led to these illegal means taking predominance in the Australian psyche. Newspapers, still now, report racing scandals as front page headlines in Australia. Recently, a ring in has been prominently featured in national newspapers. All types of racing scams are old and tested, sometimes successfully, sometimes not.

Upfield mentions some of the recent contemporary schemes of the day in relation to the action of *The Great Melbourne Cup Mystery*. In fiction, as in fact, racing scams draw high minded indignity from both the punters and owners of affected horses alike; horses are doped, people spy on horses in training, a jockey is 'taken for a ride' and horses are run 'dead'. The horses *Kambull, Gunroom* and *Cevantes*, in chapter 14 were real horses and were nobbled. Much of the contemporary flavour of Australia and Melbourne during the depression of the early 1930s is gained by the weaving of fact and fiction throughout this novel.

In 1931 Upfield left his beloved outback, where he had lived since arriving in Australia in 1910, and began living in Perth, West Australia to make his living as a writer. At the end of 1932 he was in Melbourne, Victoria working as a staff writer at *The Herald* newspaper.

By 1932 Upfield had published five novels through London publishers Hutchinson and was beginning to make a name for himself as an adequate writer of thriller and romance novels. He was becoming a well known Australian author, but the most probable reason Upfield was given a job at *The Herald* in Melbourne was that in 1932 the author had been a prominent player in a sensational murder case in West Australia.

Upfield had met a man called Snowy Rowles while working the rabbit fences of West Australia's wheat belt. Rowles used Upfield's descriptions from *The Sands of Windee* to kill two men, dispose of their bodies and steal their property. Snowy Rowles was hanged in Perth on 13 June 1932.

Newspapers serialised Upfield's novels as a lead up to the murder trial, and Upfield wrote a serialised novel, *Breakaway House* for the *Perth Mail* in 1932. At the end of 1932 Upfield was hot property for the newspapers of Australia, another novel was commissioned for serialisation. *Mr. Jelly's Business* was published in Melbourne's *The Herald* during the summer of 1932. *Mr. Jelly's Business* was the only serialised novel Upfield wrote that was published in book form during his lifetime.

The Great Melbourne Cup Mystery began its life as a newspaper serial in the spring of 1933 and remained so until re-discovered during research. Upfield had three weeks before the serial was to be published to begin the novel and it was written over the period of eight weeks (the novel was half completed when the serial began publication). Upfield was told by his editor that the novel had to encompass the Melbourne Cup and that the running of the fictional Melbourne Cup be published on the day of the 'live' race.

In the manner of his usual writing style Upfield began the novel by using his extensive knowledge of the outback and bush towns to give his fiction foundations. Mount Lion is a fictional township, and is also mentioned in the novel *The Sands of Windee*, but is based on a real township. Mount Lion can be traced to a town called Tibooburra in far western NSW, 24 miles from Milparinka. The fictional Bulka station and homestead can be traced to a station called Wompah, which lies 30 miles north east of Tibooburra. Milparinka and Wilcannia are small towns in north-western NSW, visited by the author during his days in the bush. Upfield believed in rooting his fiction to the real world, particularly since his stories were so exotic to many city dwellers.

The author then carried this process further to include fictional and non-fictional horses in the novel. The horses he mentioned as being victims of doping at Albury and Caulfield are real and contemporary of *The Great Melbourne Cup Mystery*. The other horses mentioned in the novel, with the exception of *Carbine*, are fictional. It is an important element of Upfield's fiction that he lay foundations for his novels in contemporary society. In this way Upfield mirrors some of the desperation for finding solutions to the mystery of *The Great Melbourne Cup Mystery* with actual events in Australian racing of the period.

Days before the 1930 Caulfield Cup, *Phar Lap*, that paragon of Australian champion racing horses, and his legendary companion, Tommy Woodcock, were assaulted while on an early morning walk in the streets beside the race track. Men in a large, black American car fired revolver shots to scare *Phar Lap*, when this did not work the men fired at the horse, missing it, before racing away. The culprits were never found. By April 1932 *Phar Lap* was dead in America, after convincingly winning the Aqua Caliente Handicap in Mexico. A depression affected population in Australia would never accept that *Phar Lap* had not been poisoned by interests in the American racing scene. *The Great Melbourne Cup Mystery* must have reminded a Melbourne audience, with *Phar Lap's* death a recent memory, of mysterious identities trying to control their favourite sport.

The characters of *The Great Melbourne Cup Mystery* are identifiably Upfield; full of individual idiosyncrasies to distance them from the crowd: Tom Pink, the alcoholic jockey and stuttering 'coulda been'; Old Masters, whose first name remains a mystery throughout the novel, is a gruff and affectionate man. His habit of clearing his throat is a particularly strange and unique character trait. Jack Barnett the horseman who swam three horses over a flooded creek when he couldn't swim himself, a man who would walk an acquaintance around a fire until he was blistered by its heat.

While Upfield held very strongly to the strength of individual characters in his novels they were certainly built around formulas of crime fiction of the 'Golden Age' of crime fiction; criminal masterminds and gangs hold the good folk of Melbourne in terror. Upfield works this aspect of the crime thriller with consummate irony. Mother Hubbard has her cupboard, but this cupboard is full and it reeks of a seedy and corrupt place. Not particularly nice for young children.

Tom Pink is a great ruffian character, the way he manipulates Mother Hubbard, and the way he chews off people's ears. He is one of Australian crime fictions great hero-villains; unlike Raffles, Tom Pink is firmly placed in the murky underworld of Melbourne. Tom could be accurately described as a 'terrier'—he chews ears, attacks by stealth, and does not let go. He is slightly comical, conjuring images of a small mongrel dog clinging tenaciously to the ankle of its victim.

One of Upfield's great strengths lies in his evocation of contemporary speech. All his novels reflect a commitment to recording spoken language accurately. His books describe the attitudes of these characters through what they say. Tom's language and stuttering are all rooted in the society of the 1930s, where a child's education could end as early as 12.

The Great Melbourne Cup Mystery represents a significant gap in the early novels of Upfield's work. The novel does not include Upfield's popular detective Napoleon Bonaparte but shows evidence of Upfield's early development as a writer of popular fiction. The style is coarse and fast, in keeping with the turf novel. Upfield made it, the novel was printed on time.

Stuart Mayne

DIANA ROSS

1

A Strange Side Bet

'Sorry, don't know the signature.'

'But hang it, man, I've told you I am staying with Mr Tindale, of Bulka.'

'Yes, I 'eard you, but I don't know you.'

Roy Masters, son of a wealthy Melbourne merchant, regarded the round flaming face of Mr Bumpus the hotel liscensee of Mount Lion. Here on the Mount Lion racecourse, west New South Wales, he had dropped a small bundle on a funeral hack named *Sunny Jim* and consequently now was short of ready cash when yet two races had to be run.

'Come on, Bumpus, you goin' to be all day?', drawled a lank man with a grey walrus moustache. 'Cash the gent's cheque an' get on with your job. If it was a Elder Smith cheque you'd kiss it, wouldn't you?'

'I knows their cheques,' snarled Mr Bumpus.

'A-a-nd I n-n-knows this gent is s-s-staying at Bulka,' put in a remarkably hairless person.

'There y'ar, Tom knows the gent, Bumpus. If you ain't dry. I am,' announced the walrus man.

Mr Bumpus became undecided. Anyone staying at the Bulka station most certainly was a personage, and all his life Mr Bumpus had refrained from being unobliging to personages.

'S-s-stiffen the crows, Bumpus! D-do-something,' urged the hairless one.

'Yairs, 'e wants a shot of electricity,' drawled the walrus. 'Pity 'is old woman wasn't here to liven him up.'

'Bumpus - Mr Masters' cheque will be alright,' came on steely tones from behind Roy. The man and the voice appeared to equal the voltage of the electric 'shot' prescribed by Walrus, for Mr Bumpus visably started.

'Certainly Mr Tindale, certainly,' he said hurriedly, and accepting the cheque with a smirk, he dashed for the cash register.

'Hey! Kiss that cheque afore you put it away,' Walrus implored, thereby raising general laughter, during which Roy turned to his host.

'Thanks. I'd run out of cash and on your advice I applied to Mr Bumpus,' he said.

'I should have given you a chit.' The pale lean face of one of the wealthiest squatters of western New South Wales broke into a slow smile, and the slate-blue eyes twinkled. 'There are more goats – animals not men – in Mount Lion than Treasury notes. You see, our general currency is in cheque. Yes, Bumpus! Two guggle-guggles, please.'

'What is your opinion of *Better 'Ole* in the next race?' Roy asked.

'So so. Anything will win,' Tindale prophesied, stroking his short iron-grey moustache whilst calmly examining the dark alert face beside him. The liquor 'guggled' whilst it flowed from the bottle he held. 'I feel more confident, however, that my own horse will not win the last race.'

'Oh! I thought he looked a better stayer than *Darling*.'

'Granted, but he's not up to his true form today. And

2

Darling's appearances are deceptive. As a matter of fact, I have just backed *Darling* for a small amount.'

'It doesn't seem much good backing anything,' Roy stated impatiently. 'You can never get a decent odds at these country meetings.'

'No, but we get a lot of fun,' the squatter pointed out. 'Up here we attend the races in a holiday spirit, we do not regard racing as a serious business.'

Roy chuckled when they turned from the bar.

'I can agree with you on that point. Seen Dick lately?'

Mr Tindale was lighting a cigarette, which may have accounted for the distinct pause, before saying:

'I left him taking to Diana in the stand. Alverey was with them, yet seemed to be not of them.'

'Ah! Well - perhaps it is none of my business, Mr Tindale, but am I right in understanding that Alverey proposed to Diana a few days ago?'

'He did. The foolish maid rejected him.'

'Why foolish? He's devilish handsome and all that, but - well - he's not British, you know.'

'Dear me!' sighed the older man. 'Dear me! Rabid nationalism appears to be increasing everywhere. The fact that Alverey is a foreigner cannot be held against him, whilst entirely in his favor is the fact that he is worth four millions in pounds, not dollars, or francs, or cents.'

Roy's murmured exclamations inferred disagreement, and, another man claiming his host's attention, he slipped away to rejoin his friend of years and the girl he loved.

Again in the brilliant May sunshine he had completely forgotten the coming race and *Better 'Ole*, even though the four bookmakers were shouting the horse's name. He was too absorbed to hear the shouted odds, the dull persistent roar of the crowd. His mind was too occupied with what Tindale had said about Diana and Dick and about Alverey, who, although with them, seemed to inhabit the chilly world in which lived all third parties. Yes, it was necessary to know at once, if Dick actually loved Diana.

Two years had Dick and he intimately known Diana, Mr Tindale's ward, and heiress to a fortune created from the China trade. Most successfully had the squatter hidden this splendid specimen of Australian beauty; as it were, producing her to Melbourne society, and the public in general, per the medium of the illustrated weeklies, after her education had been completed and he had conducted her on a world tour.

That was when Diana was twenty-one and from the evening Dick and he had been presented to her at a ball, he had loved her. And Dick – jovial old Dick – did he love her too? Strong friends though they long had been, his love for Diana had been a thing too sacred to discuss with his friend. And now Alverey was with Diana and Dick, yet seemed not of them. Depression rested heavily on him, and then, when a cheery voice spoke against his ear, strangely lifted.

'What are you going to back in this one,' demanded, rather than asked, a powerfully built man some twenty-seven years old, a man whose face was square, whose features were rugged, whose eyes were a violet-blue and whose hair was auburn.

Roy said, seriously:

'Nothing, Dick. But I want to talk to you about a subject of greater consequence than backing a horse. Let's find a quiet place. Come on - they're off and we haven't much time before the last race is run.'

4

'Are you going to plank your entire time doings on the last race?' asked Dick, again like a demand, his eyes reflecting the gaity of the crowd; his hair reflecting the sunlight, his plain face reflecting the buoyancy of his soul.

Not answering his friend, Roy gripped Dick's arm above the elbow and led him to a place temporarily vacated by people who had hurried to the grandstand to view the race. And then, in his direct fashion, he said quiely:

'I want you to tell me if you love Diana.'

For two seconds Dick's underjaw sagged. The light in his eyes dimmed and he answered the question in the affirmative by merely nodding. Roy stared with unseeing eyes at the short band of colours sweeping into the straight. Then quite abruptly he turned square to his friend.

'We've been friends a long time now,' he said slowly. 'I hope we will never fall out over Diana.'

Dick's eyes narrowed.

'Do you think there is any probability of our falling out?' he asked in tones which did not make his question a demand.

'It is hard to give an opinion. History is full of cases of two friends loving the same woman with disasterous results to their friendship.'

'Not with us. We've been pals too long. If you love Diana, too, then we'll play fair. What the hell are we going to do about it?'

'Have you proposed to her?'

'No,' replied Dick. 'I had a chance to in the stand a little while ago, but Alverey butted in. I might punch him on the nose yet.'

'Well he's making the pace and we have to keep up,' Roy said determinedly. 'We have got to decide the matter as far as we are concerned before the house-party breaks up to-morrow.'

'All right. You box on. If Diana doesn't accept you, I'll try my luck and I reckon my luck is as good as Alverey's, despite his money.'

'No, I'm not going to accept priority like that,' stated Roy firmly. 'I'll tell you what we'll do. In the next race, the last this meeting, there are only two horses running, the third having been scratched.

'We'll each back one of those horses and the winner entitles his backer to propose first go to Diana.'

'Fair enough,' agreed Dick Cusack. 'Let's see: *Paroo*, Tindale's horse, is running. Which one is scratched?'

'*Black Lucy.*'

'Good! Leaving *Darling*, owned by Smith. How do we pick 'em?'

'Put the names in a hat and draw them, if you like.'

'Do me. We'll do it now - and no squealing from the loser as usual.'

'Of course not, Dick. If you win, I'll be your best man.'

'Same here,' Dick agreed readily, whilst Roy hastily wrote the names on two strips of paper torn from his note-book.

Roy drew Mr Tindale's horse, *Paroo*. He was sincerely pleased that Dick would get the first chance, for had not *Paroo*'s owner said he had backed darling?

'And that's that,' Dick said briskly. 'I don't know one horse from t'other, but I'm backing my luck.'

2

When You Are Ready

Diana Ross, radiantly flushed with excitement, for at twenty-three few girls are incapable of being thrilled even by second rate horses running a race, sat surrounded by her friends and her guardian's guests of whom only Roy was absent. Senor Alverey was saying in his peculiar English:

'But two horses, eh? The winner of thees race so easy to, what you say, find?'

'Yes. Mr. Tindale's horse, *Paroo*, is to win this race,' announced Smith, the secretary to the Mount Lion Jockey Club. He was short and tubby, and his face was round and shining, yet a poker face. Confidently he added: 'The horses have arranged it between them.'

'A-ah! But was it not your so great general, Wellington, who said so sublimely: "It is all horses which are liars"?'

Above the laughter in which the dark, handsome senor heartily joined, Mr. Tindale was heard to say calmly:

'*Darling* will have to be mighty slow if she loses to *Paroo* after my animal's performance in the Stakes.'

'Oh, he didn't do badly, guardie. He gained third place,' Diana exclaimed with a partially bestowed smile on all. 'You can't expect the poor dear to win every time.'

'Well, I expected him to win that time, anyway.'

'You think he not win thees race, Mistaire Tindale?'

'Not even in face of what the horses have arranged. Beside *Paroo* hasn't a Tom Pink on his back.'

'I love that man,' asserted Diana with much conviction.

'I don't,' Tom Pink's employer stated emphatically.

'But he's such an original type,' the girl argued mischievously. 'A thorough Jekyll-Hyde man. On the ground he is like a crab. On a horse he's like—like part of the horse.'

'I grant he is all right when he's on a saddle, Miss Ross,' was Smith's grudging surrender, 'but he's old enough not to stutter and splutter when he talks to you. I don't mind a shower before breakfast, but ...'

'You can't expect all things of a good rider,' Mr. Tindale pointed out, in which he was backed by the Argentinian.

'No, he is a ver' good rider, not a, what you call heem, a— a gate cracker.'

'Still, for all that I'm not paying him to replace my shower bath,' the secretary bitterly complained. 'I've just come from telling him to ride his best, and I've made my mind never to talk to him again unless he's sitting on a horse.'

'But he cannot always be sitting on a horse,' Diana pointed out, rising to her feet and trying hard not to giggle. Then, imperiously to Senor Alverey: 'Please put this pound on *Paroo* for me.'

'Sairtenly, Meese Ross,' Alverey said, taking the proffered note with a bow that only the Latin can execute superbly. 'I? I will follow your star. Twenty bills will I put on heem, too?'

Diana noted the dark eyes flashing from his dark, handsome face. There were moments when she thought she liked him immensely, and Alverey as quick to sense these transitory phases which gave him confidence that sooner or later he would win her.

The object of Diana's mirth and Mr. Smith's well-grounded complaint, was he who seconded Roy's statement in the bar that he was one of Mr. Tindale's guests. A remarkable man, Tom Pink, in more than appearance. Even those people capable of guessing how many peas there are in a bottle, those shrewd men able to guess the dead weight of a beast, would have found difficulty in judging Tom's age. His legs were too short for the length of his body, and his hands were too big for the size of this arms. The sleeves of the black and gold shirt he wore were rolled to his arm-pits, and when he removed his white cap to scratch his head it was seen that he was completely bald. He was an old young man, yet there was no accounting for this, for the one ruling passion of his life was horses.

'I reckon we'll be going,' he said to Mr. Tindale's rider, in a slow rolling drawl.

'Yass, let's. Old Bicton 'as bin at the barrier ten minutes.'

As though two stockmen starting off for the days muster, so did Tom and Lew Jackson ride away to the barrier in this seven-furlong contest. And on the way to the irate starter, Tom said casually:

'Well—I'm on a dead 'un.'

It appeared that Lew Jackson required time mentally to assimilate this statement of fact, for a time-space of ten seconds elapsed before he said:—

'Are yous. Well, I'm on a dead 'un, too.'

'You don't say,' Tom remarked casually.

'I do say.'

'We can't both ride dead 'uns.'

'No—but I'm ridin' the one dead.'

'But you can't be, 'cos I'm ridin' it.'

'You ain't. I got strict instructions from old Tindale to ride this disjointed cow as dead as mutton. An' Tindale's the president of the club.'

'An' Smithy is the secretary,' Tom stated, as though he imparted a close guarded stable secret.

''E says: "Tom," 'e says, "you will not ride *Darling* to win this race." Wot's more Lew, I am obeying owners orders.'

'So'm I.'

During the remainder of the short journey to the barrier these two were silent, even when Mr. Bicton, the starter addressed them like an admiral from his quarter-deck. Starting with his hand on the gate gear roundly cursed all unpunctual persons in idiom betraying the sea-faring career of his youth.

The two horses were brought up to the barrier, when Tom with offside instep pressure spun *Darling* right round. *Darling* was so astonished she reacted and would have plunged away back to the grandstand had not his rider controlled the impulse with hands of steel.

This made Lew's bay gelding more anxious than ever to get away. For a second time they faced up to the barrier, and this time *Darling*, who took outside place, side-stepped smartly and badly bumped her fretting opponent.

'Ain't the world big enough?' Lew snarled.

'Come 'ere, you,' drawled Tom to *Darling*, and edged her off the gelding then to knee his mount round to take the backward plunge once more.

Mr. Bicton, who always carried with him a patent shooting stool opened it with studied deliberation and as deliberately sat down.

'Just when you are ready,' he roared in tones more insulting than a language he sometimes used.

By this time *Paroo* was giving her rider much trouble, whilst Lew Jackson's rising anger, becoming communicated to the horse, increased the animal's impatience to be away.

'Now, if you gentlemen have made up your minds to start we'll weigh anchor,' announced Mr. Bicton, standing up. And then, as the horses were both facing the barrier, although several yards from it, the starter swung up the gate and yelled:

'Let go - let go, you flaming horse marines.'

Suprised by this procedure, the jockeys looked at one another for a fleeting second, when *Paroo* almost took the bit in his mouth and bolted. With the yells of execration vented by the starter, thundering in his ears, Tom Pink permitted *Darling* to follow, and *Darling*, not having been used to being in that state known as dead, determined to catch up.

Ahead, some four or five lengths *Paroo* moved along at easy speed. With his huge hands as light as feathers and as strong as iron clamps, Tom permitted his bewildered mare to creep up. Never before had he passed so slowly the little white posts marking the inside of the course.

Now and then Lew Jackson, who had *Paroo* well under control by that time glanced back at Tom and noted the grin on Tom's face.

'I'm ridin' a dead 'un,' he yelled. 'Come on up. This is the presidents horse.'

'I'm ridin' the sec's horse, an he's as dead as beef. Go on—you're doin' alright,' screamed Tom, never before so like the Tom Pink on the ground.

Half way to the post the two horses were moving at little

more than a canter. Their riders could hear the roar of the spectators, and neither found difficulty in understanding the reason for it.

Now, but a short distance ahead of them Tom could see the ornamental post marking that flank of the inside railings which ran to the same distance beyond the stand. Slower and yet slower galloped the horses. Each jockey was lying along his animal's neck as though in the final burst of speed. Tom was raising and lowering his whip on pretence of thrashing the mare, but not once did he strike her.

Neck and neck they turned into the straight, restraining bits in the mouths of anxious horses covering their riders with snow. On the inside, suddenly *Paroo* faltered, half reared, and ran off the course round the end of the inside railings.

Tom Pink had the course to himself.

Hilarious cat-calls, yells and groans, laughter and imprecations greeted him when *Paroo*, indignantly yet superbly, trotted like an old cavalry charger slowly past the stand to the winning post.

This bush crowd accepted the farce in a sporting spirit. Men shouted with laughter and slapped each other on the back until their eyes watered—women laughing more shrilly but with less physical exuberance. When Tom Pink having dismounted, was met by Mr. Smith he saw that his employer's face was white with rage.

'Didn't I tell you not to win the race?' demanded the secretary with lowered voice.

'Y-y-yes, you did,' stuttered Tom, almost blinding Mr. Smith. Like a ripple caused by a stone flung into still water, so from that point expanded a wave which silenced the crowd. Even from the far end of the grandstand people could hear

Tom Pink disclaiming:

'Y-y-yes, you told me to r-r-ride 'im dead. I rid 'im dead. I c-c-couldn't have rid 'im no deader, c-c-could I? But Lew was on a dead 'un, too. An' 'e rid *Paroo* dead. Dead - deader'n I rode *Darling*. Only two 'orses and them r-r-rid as dead as door-nails, one 'ad to win, didn't he? 'Ow was I t-t-to know Lew would turn off the flamin' course? T-t-tell me that!'

The distance defying voice died away, and there burst out a great sound of laughter which swelled into deep-throated mirth. And when the race was declared no race and all bets were cancelled, the throng streamed away to the parked motor cars and trucks and tethered horses still in great glee.

It was arranged between the two friends that Dick Cusack should persuade Diana to return to Bulka with him in his single-seater, and thus take the opportunity to propose, which Roy insisted was his right.

SENOR ALVEREY & DIANA ROSS

3

A Sporting Run

For mid-May the night was warm, sufficiently warm to dictate open windows, and towards midnight Roy and Dick, who occupied the same bedroom at Bulka, were lounging therein, in dressing gown and slippers. Although each knew that the opportunity to propose to Diana had been offered to the other, not until now did they compare notes with the freedom of old friends.

'Well - how did you get on?' inquired Roy, after a short silence, during which the lightly-falling rain on shrubs and earth sent a message of good promise drifting in through the wide french windows.

'A complete thud,' Dick replied, vulgarly explicit.

'And you?'

'Ditto.'

Another short period of silence, spent in moody smoking. Then:

'Diana said she was sorry, but she didn't love me,' Dick explained, with an unusually glum expression. 'I suppose she said that to you, too?'

Roy nodded.

'Did she tell you, too, that the man she married would have to have done something worthwhile in the world?'

'Yes. Something wonderful like building a great railway

or a bridge or being a famous statesman. She pointed to Alverey as a shining example.'

'Lovely, isn't it?' Dick growled. 'Here are you helping your Dad to run a mammoth business in Melbourne and umpteen branches throughout Victoria and here's me running sixty thousand sheep in the Riverina, and 'cos neither of us are bloomin' politicians we cut no ice.'

'She gave me a wee chance, or what she called a wee chance,' Roy answered.

'Oh - did she? Did she tell you she would marry you within a month if one of your mokes won the Melbourne Cup?'

'She gave me that wee chance.'

'It's so wee that I canna see it. Can you?'

'No. And yet—'

'What?' Dick vigorously tossed the end of his cigarette through the open windows. The glowing butt described an arc over the verandah and its low balustrade to fall into the garden beyond. Whilst not directly in the light, Dick could see a black cat crouched on the balustrade. It was slowly rising to its full height, when its back became arched and it softly spat. 'What were you going to say, Roy?'

'That we might give the Melbourne Cup a fly.'

'What with? None of our stuff has a single hair of a Cup winner sticking out of him.'

'Nevertheless, we'll give it a fly.'

During the full following minute neither spoke; Roy earnestly regarding his friend, whilst Dick almost sub-consciously watched the cat, and for the first time in his life not being thrilled by falling rain after a long dry period.

'Well, what are we going to do about it?' persisted the

younger man.

'About what?' countered Dick.

'About the Melbourne Cup.'

'Oh! I was thinking of Alverey. Oh, yes, I suppose you could run *Olary Boy* and I could enter *Pieface*, but we'll have to get busy and hire a gang of good horse-dopers.'

'What for?'

'Why - because every other galloper in the race will have to be doped if one of our horses is to win it.'

'It is too early to know just what *Pieface* and *Olary Boy* might do. If it should rain the night before, *Olary Boy* would be suited. As four-year-olds both might do exceptionally well this winter and spring.'

'They'd have a wee chance, as Diana said,' Dick snorted.

'Still, a chance Dick,' Roy further persisted. 'I've had a good offer for *Olary Boy*, as you know. I told Sparks to sell at noon tomorrow if he didn't hear from me. I'll write him in the morning not to sell. Diana is right after all. We haven't done much in the world bar spend money we do not really earn. Come, let's give Diana's offer a sporting run.'

Instead of at once vigorously backing this suggestion, Dick Cusack lit another cigarette, then to slump deeper into his chair. The cat was again arching its back and softly spitting. It actually was annoyed with him.

'What is the good, Roy? Just suppose we were able to find a crook keen enough to dope every other horse but ours. Supposin' *Olary Boy* or *Pieface* won the Cup? What do we do then? The winner takes it to Diana saying: 'Here Diana take the cocktail shaker for the sideboard. Through my horse I have done a great and noble deed. My name is in all the papers. As per contract, red ink the wedding day.' So far everything would be O.K. But winning the Cup isn't going to create love in Diana's heart for the winner, and I'm in love with Diana to the extent that I wouldn't want her to marry me if she didn't love me as much as I love her. Get me, Roy?'

During this quite lucid presentation of their case, the cat had again sunk down to the verandah rail.

Continuing idly to watch the cat, Dick heard Roy present the case from a different angle.

'There is logic in what you have said, old man. That is, logic from your viewpoint. But let us adopt the argument, or basis of argument, that Colonel Swinton put into a short story I think he called "The Green Curve". That is about two opposing generals in a war. The general who won was he who successfully anticipated how his opponent was thinking and deciding his tactics accordingly.'

'Well - what have generals got to do with our winning the Melbourne Cup to oblige a lady?' Dick cut in observing with a shade more interest the cat outside on the verandah rail, again standing up and slowly arching its back.

'This. Let us ask ourselves why Diana after having said she loved neither of us, set us a seemingly impossible task. I believe if she had been sure she didn't love one of us she would not have given us the "wee chance". The Melbourne Cup is six months ahead. Diana, I think, gave us a "wee chance" in order to give herself six months' time to make up her mind.'

'About what?'

'Which one of us she loves.'

'Meaning that in six months time she will know her own mind.'

'Just that. She knows we have as much chance of winning

the Cup as we have of marrying into royalty. She realises that there will be no chance of you, for instance, snaffling the Cup and she finding out she loves me; or vice versa. If and when she does find out which of us she cares for, trust her – or any other woman – to convey the intelligence.'

'Well, what do we do?' he demanded.

'We will try and get the Cup.'

'But we haven't a hope.'

'We'll try nevertheless.'

Yet again the cat was slowly arching its back. Dick Cusack, still idly watching it, pressed the catch of his petrol lighter, brought the flame against the end of his third cigarette. The weed alight, still without definite purpose, he lowered the lighter a few inches, when the little flame revealed the cat on the rail several degrees clearer. The cat was in the act of hissing - not at him.

'I'll stop the sale of *Olary Boy* tomorrow,' Roy went on. 'We'll put our other mokes away, and concentrate on these possible but not probable Melbourne Cup winners. We'll give the Cup a fly. If all the other acceptances for the race should perish of cold and one of our mokes manage to get around the winning post, we'll both go to Diana and say: "We don't hold you to your promise, because neither of us expected to get the gee-gaw. Forget it. If you still think you love neither one, hurry and say so, please. If you know you love one of us hurry ever so much more to say so. The loser will not squeal."'

'Good egg! I'm game,' Dick agreed, standing up. 'I think - I'll take a walk!'

He took a short spring, vaulted the windowsill, landed like a cat in the verandah, as lightly as the actual cat fled, spun to his right and so came face to face with Senor Alverey, who stood with his back against the house wall but a foot to one side of the window frame.

'Beautiful night, isn't it - for spies,' Dick drawled dangerously low. 'Come right in and have a little talk.'

'I was but just passing, Mistaire Cusack.'

'You don't say! Well - come in'

Senor Jose Alverey, still arrayed in immaculate dinner dress, was gripped by the silk lapels of his coat and almost lifted from his feet right into the bedroom.

'I never did have very much time for you, friend Josey, and just now I have no time at all for you,' Dick stated grittily.

'I was, I can assure, just passing.'

'The cat on the balustrade proves you a liar.'

'You call me a liar?'

'Too right.'

Alverey sprang into the air at the instant he attempted to strike. It was, however, an unsuccessful attempt, because a short arm uppercut sent him sprawling on to Roy's bed.

'Now get out before I help you in your going.'

Alverey's dark face was like that of a corpse.

'You will regret,' he managed to jerk out. 'You win the Melbourne Cup with your, what you say? — your down-on-the-feet cab horses.' His white hands became fluttering wings. 'We will wait. We will see. I crush you. You insult, you strike me, eh? You call me Josey! Bah!'

'See my boots anywhere, Roy? These felt slippers are no good,' Dick said plaintively.

evidently didn't like Alverey. Toast?'

'Confound the rain.'

'Tut-tut. Blessed be the rain,' Dick said reprovingly. 'Every drop means a penny to the station hand, a zac to the manger, fourpence to the squatter, and twenty-five bob to the government.'

'I have no doubt you are right,' Roy said, attempting sarcasm, 'but I don't like the prospect of driving a car thirty odd miles through this rain.'

'Don't worry. You'll not be driving any car thirty odd miles through this rain, Roy.'

'But, I'll have to if they can't get the 'phone line repaired.'

Dick shook his head. 'There will be no driving of motor cars about the landscape today. Three hundred and seventeen points of rain have already fallen.'

'But I've got to get that telegram away even if ten inches fall between now and when I start after I've eaten.'

Diana entered, as freshly and lovely as though she had slept for ten hours.

'Morning everyone,' she greeted the half-dozen at the table. 'Isn't the rain splendid? We are water-locked, and no-one will be able to leave today, at least. What say we arrange a bridge tournament?'

'But mother and I will have to go. We simply must catch the Adelaide express from Broken Hill tonight,' exclaimed a pretty brunette. 'We promised faithfully to be at Bobbie Culbert-Smithson's wedding tomorrow.'

'Bobbie will have to get married without your blessing, Eva,' Dick cut in.

'But why? Why? Why?'

'Yes, why?' added Roy.

'Because on these north-western tracks a baby's pram would be hopelessly bogged in the first mile. What is it from here to Mount Lion? Thirty-two miles, and one hundred and sixty miles on top of that to Broken Hill. Nope - we play bridge, Eva, all day long. And, perhaps, all day tomorrow, too.'

'I'm so glad,' Diana said impishly.

Breakfast over Roy and Dick made for the office. Mr. Keen rang up Mount Lion and failed to raise the exchange.

'Well, I've got to get a telegram away,' Roy persisted, adding to the squatter: 'What do you think about it? Dick says it is impossible to reach Mount Lion today by car.'

'Dick's right, Roy,' corroborated Mr. Tindale.

'What about horses and buckboard?'

'Saddle horses would get further than a buckboard, but Red Creek will be in roaring flood. Why, this is the best rain we've had in these parts for three years or more.'

'There is no centre we could ring up other than Mount Lion?'

'None. Your business terrifically important?'

'Yes, very. I had arranged with my trainer to sell a horse of mine if I did not cancel the arrangement by noon today. I've altered my mind. I simply cannot let the horse go. What other township is near here?'

'Milparinka - forty-six miles distant.'

'There is no point we could reach from which a 'phoned telegram could be sent to Milparinka?'

'Yes. You could 'phone a message from Moorabbin Station homestead thirty-eight miles from here. But understand, Roy, all the creeks will be running bankers. I am afraid there is nothing you can do to save your horse from sale - unless the line break is discovered and repaired in time this morning.'

With vexed impatience Roy paced the length of the office, Dick meanwhile studying a survey map of the district hanging on the wall.

'Could a saddle horse make the trip?' he demanded, swinging round to the squatter.

'I much doubt it. A lot of swimming would have to be done.'

'Would you lend me a good hack?' Roy further demanded.

'Yes, but you would be foolish to undertake the trip.'

'No matter. I'll try it. Order me a horse, Mr. Tindale, please, and let me start at once. There is not a minute to waste.'

'All right. Fix it, Miles,' the squatter asked his manager. 'You can get the Ten-mile, can't you, Keen?'

'Yes, the break is beyond that.'

'Good! Ring them up and tell them to have a saddle horse they've got there ready for Mr. Masters. And say I would like one of them to accompany Mr. Masters as far as Red Creek.'

'I'll change,' Roy snapped, hurrying out.

'Think he'll do it?' questioned Dick.

'I don't, but he seems determined to try it,' Mr. Tindale replied grimly, and Dick fell again to studying the survey map.

Five minutes dragged on before Roy re-entered. The bookkeeper made another attempt to get through to Mount Lion and failed.

'I see they've saddled a horse for me. I'll be off,' announced Roy. 'Here is the telegram I want sent. Keep trying to get through in case I don't reach Mount Lion on time.'

'All right. Now get this information clear,' the squatter snapped. 'Mount Lion from here is almost south-west. The first ten miles will be fair going and you won't lose the track. You will then arrive at one of our huts named the Ten-mile. We have two riders living there and they will have a horse ready for you. From the Ten-mile to Red Creek is eleven miles, the worst stretch of the journey. One of the Ten-mile men will accompany you as far as Red Creek, because you will be unable to follow the road in places and will be apt to miss it. Should you get across Red Creek you will find the remaining eleven miles easy to trace, for you will then be in the gibber uplands. If you should determine to cross Red Creek, please don't ask the Ten-mile man to accompany you, because he's a good sheep man and I don't want him drowned. Now - get away and the best of luck.'

'Thank you,' Roy said quietly. 'So long, Dick.'

'So long, Roy, and good luck,' Dick replied absently.

5

In A Hurry

At the beginning of a ride he never was to forget, Roy Masters had no little difficulty in managing the dapple-grey gelding which the manager had selected for him, but when once the powerful horse warmed up he moved like a well-oiled machine.

In less than two minutes Roy was saturated with water. It drove against him from the rear off-side, heavy sheets of rain flung forward by a tempestuous north-west wind. His world was wind-lashed mulga and sandalwood trees growing on undulating red sand-covered country from which the last summer's sun had scorched all herbage. In and out among the higher ridges wound the narrow track easily discernible despite the wind, for the rain had arrived several hours before the tempest.

What was it? What had Tindale said? Easy going to the stockman's hut at the Ten-mile. Then eleven bad miles; then Red Creek, which apparently was supposed to stop him. After that, eleven more miles, comparatively easier.

But he must not delude himself that he was in for an easy ride. Without doubt he could push his grey over the ten miles to the hut, but the horse he obtained there, no matter how good, would have to be ridden carefully the remaining twenty-two miles.

When through the first gate, three miles on his way, he walked the horse for half a mile. His hat had been blown from his head and he had not turned back to rescue it. Steam from the gelding drifted away to the near side, but of the two living things in that world of falling water the horse was the least discomforted.

Then on again at an easy canter until stopped by a wide box-lined creek down which ran a surging mass of water. Yet here was small danger, a creek not worth mentioning by the squatter. As, indeed, was it, for it is the narrow creek which runs deep.

They must have crossed half the distance to the Ten-mile. Five miles! Thirty-two, less five, was twenty-seven, and those twenty-seven speedometer-measured miles to be crossed before half-past eleven at the latest. He knew Sparks well enough to be sure that he wouldn't clinch the deal one second before twelve o'clock. And because Nat Sparks thought a lot of *Olary Boy*, it was likely that he would delay the business thirty minutes, or even an hour, hoping to receive orders to cancel the sale.

An ugly brute, *Olary Boy*. Roman nose; thick legs. A clothes prop of a horse to look at. He could run a bit, to be sure, but in appearance no credit either to owner or trainer. Yet for all that, he was a fool to part with *Olary Boy*. Yes, a fool too, to feel annoyed because a girl, when she first saw the horse, laughed at *Olary Boy's* disreputable appearance. Sired by a Caulfield Cup winner, too, and out of a mare who had raced well at the many provincial meetings in her day. Well, they couldn't always breed 'em up. And as a yearling the moke suggested no throw back.

The ground was slipping away beneath the gelding's feet.

He was beginning to blow a little. But he would be blowing a bit harder when they reached the Ten-mile.

'Come on - get on with it,' Roy cried, and for the first time, touched the animal's flanks with his spurless boot-heels.

The grey responded well, indicating plenty of reserve. The country now was gathered into wide spaced, but steeper, sand-ridges running east and west. The track angled up one side of every ridge and angled down the other, the long narrow flats between composed of sticky chocolate-coloured soil bearing saltbrush.

The rain continued steadily. The wind was veering slowly westward, coming to send the stinging raindrops against the rider's right cheek. The horse galloped without apparently tiring, but his chest was heaving, his nostrils widely showing pink, and his body steamed.

And thus unexpectedly they reached the southern most rampart of sand, to see from its summit the rain-dulled picture of a little iron hut on the far side of a small treeless plain.

'Now for it, old boy,' Roy shouted, and urged his mount with heels and open hand. In a grand final burst of speed the gelding crossed the mile-wide plain to pull up with heaving flanks and drooping head.

Two saddled horses and one horse bridled only were tethered to a horse rail in the lee of the hut. Two men in rough overcoats ran out of the crazy structure, one to take over the dappled gelding. Said to the other:

'You've made good time. The boss has just rung up. They still can't get through to Mount Lion. We've made a cupper tea. 'Ave a drink before we push on?'

'Yes, I'll spare one minute,' Roy agreed. And then, when

inside the hut and sipping tea alternately munching brownie whilst standing before the great fire in the open hearth: 'Three horses ready. Both you fellows coming with me?'

'No, I'm going with you as far as Red Crick. I'm taking a spare 'orse for you to change over when we git there. None of 'em ain't no *Carbines*, but they can travel faster than *Darling* when Tom rid 'im parst the grandstand yesterdee. I bin laffin' all night about it.'

'Were you there?'

'Too right. Fred an' me went in on his ole truck.'

'Well, we'd better go,' Roy decided, draining the tea in his tin pint pannikin.

'Righto!' and the stockman began to remove his overcoat.

'You'se gonna git wet, Jack,' prophesied the man referred to by Jack as Fred.

'Too right, I'm gonna git wet. But that bleeding overcoat's gonna weigh ten pounds or more when she gits full of rain,' Jack drawled in the unhurried manner of the bushman.

Now mounted on a spirited black filly, Roy was made thankful that the saddle he bestrode was older than that in which he had ridden from the homestead, softer and much more comfortable. He was not used to riding as he might have been had not motor cars been invented. Even the short rest after a mere ten miles canter-cum-gallop revealed his softness.

'We'll being following the road for the first four miles,' the stockman explained whilst the three horses cantered abreast. After that you'll 'ave to foller me 'cos I'll be winding about orl over the scenery to reach easy crossings over about two thousand and seven 'undred cricks. You in a 'urry to see your mother-in-law planted or what?'

'No,' Roy replied, laughingly. 'No. I'm in a hurry to stop my trainer from selling one of my horses which I have decided to run for the Melbourne Cup.'

'Oh - what's 'is chances? Wot's 'is name?'

'His name is *Olary Boy* and his chances are nil.'

'You don't say. Lemme think,' Jack fell to thinking with one eye closed tight. 'He won the Mentone Welter Handicap, First Divi, last year, didn't he?'

'Yes.'

'Yairs. Lemme think again. Yairs. I backed *Fairy Queen* both ways that race and dropped a fiver.'

And incessantly talking about horses they reached that point on the journey where they were to lose the road.

'Now yer foller me,' Jack directed. 'We'll keep 'em goin' hard for another mile and they'll get a breather for a coupler miles.'

Abruptly the country changed from yielding sand to more yielding grey flats on which grew stunted, warped and shrivelled looking box timber. Roy was obliged to ease his mount further back in order to escape the rain of mud thrown up by the two horses in front. They crossed places covered with thin sheets of water in great plunging strides; over other places as slippery as grease on which the animals slithered badly.

The wind was losing its boisterousness, and the rain was becoming less heavy the further the wind veered southward. A line of bigger timber ahead presently introduced them to a creek in which was ugly foaming water, water flowing as beer might flow from a bombarded brewery.

'Let 'em take their time, Mr. Masters,' shouted Jack. 'They've all crosted it before and they will again.'

As was quite evident when the three animals faced that raging stream without hesitation. But shallow storm-water always is ugly in comparison to the deep and placid and smooth water in which milling currents lie concealed. The water at this crossing barely reached to the horses' girths.

As Jack had intimated, for two miles they were compelled to walk their mounts, winding about between deep gutter and deeper creeks in which water had not run for many months.

A veritable maze, Jack led the way without fault across this wide strip of flood country, the horses being taxed to their utmost by glutinous mud compelling frequent halts to remove hardening balls of mud from hoofs.

'Orstralia! Well - when they says it's sunny, they're liars, and when they say it's dry, they're liars,' was Jack's comment offered more than once.

'Let's push on,' Roy constantly urged.

'Oh, yairs, and blow out these animiles before we hit Red Crick. Leave it ter me. Another mile or thereabouts and we come ter sand country again.'

The enforced slowness of the pace was irksome to the younger man, now desperately anxious to save his horse from sale. The wind was less boisterous, but the rain continued. Saturated with water, their clothes clung to them with the chill touch of snakes. Their hands were blue with the cold. Roy was finding it the most wretched journey he ever had undertaken, but Jack maintained unquenchable cheerfulness.

At last! The dunes of the sand country could be seen

between the trunks of the weird box trees appearing like animate objects convulsed in final death struggles; and, arriving on the clean land, for the last time they removed the caked mud from the twelve equine feet.

'Give 'em a blow; they'll pay it back,' Jack urged. 'I'm makin' a cigarette anyway; I can't breathe for want of a gasper. Have one?'

Roy nodded and fell to swinging his arms to create bodily warmth.

'She's a corker this rain,' Jack gabbled on whilst crouched in the lee of a cotton bush to protect papers and matches and tobacco he carried in an air-tight tin. Blue eyes contrasted vividly in a face blackened by sun and wind. 'It reminds me of the time me and Tom Pink got on the drunk at Bourke back in twenty-two. The more we drank the higher Tom's voice got, and the more he stuttered. The police give us the oil to get out of town, and we buys a boat so's we could have a quiet holiday floatin' down the river. We anchors one night two miles above Menindie, and swore we wouldn't go ashore there 'cos we'd decided to visit Tom's uncle wot owns a grape plot at Mildura. But during the night the boat anchor come unstuck or somethink. We're sleepin' in the boat, and when we wakes there's the ole boat trying to get into the back door of the Menindie Hotel, the tide was that high. Come on - we'll be goin'.'

Now at a hard gallop they bore southward over a wide rib of sand-covered country where the wind had fashioned grotesque pillars and cliffs and houses from the harder lumps. Roy saw that once more they were on the road, and presently cresting a rise saw, too, beyond a strip of claypan country, a line of red gums which evidently marked the course of Red Creek.

They arrived at Red Creek at twenty to eleven.

And above the hiss of the wind through the red gums they heard a man crying desperately for help.

ROY MASTERS

6

A Man And Three Horses

Blood! Bright fresh blood, sixty yards in width, sliding by. Against the banks, against trees, which have fallen inward from the banks, and against an island of debris almost in the middle of the stream and higher than the normal crossing, blood-tinged foam clung, as though this channel drained the blood of some vast battlefield, not the red flats westward.

And on the island of debris composed of ancient tree snags and gnarled branches, a man submerged to his neck in this river of blood.

'Hey! Wa'cher doin' there, Tom?' Jack shouted, then to add to Roy: 'Why it's ole Tom Pink.'

'Help me – I can't hang on much longer. I can't feel nothing. I bin 'ere for hours. I can't swim - I can't swim.'

'Cripes! First time I ever 'eard him not stutterin' off'n a 'orse. What are we gonna do, mister?' casually inquired the stockman.

'Get him out. We must do something,' Roy said rapidly, the urgent necessity of quickly reaching Mount Lion temporarily forgotten. 'Can you swim?'

'No, curse it, I can't.'

Roy began to tear off his sodden clothes, and Jack, seeing his purpose, shouted to Tom encouragingly:

'It'll be orl right, Tom. Here's a gent comin' in for you. 'Ow did you git there? Jew fly, or was you paddling a tree trunk acrost?'

'I was ridin' me 'orse further up an' we got tangled in a snag under water. I got throwed off and I'd a drownded if I adn't come against this snag 'ere.'

Roy ran upstream, observing the glassy surface of this dreadful water, to ascertain where hidden snags might lie. He saw two patches of troubled surface, and saw how he must swim to avoid the jagged teeth of wood below them.

With a prayer to Dame Fortune, he jumped feet first into the flood. No dim light of translucent water welcomed him in the depths. An inky blackness enveloped him, and when again he met the blessed light of day, his eyes and mouth were level with an ice-cold crimson sheet. The trees on either bank were rushing by. Momentarily he glimpsed Jack dancing like an idiot. The island of debris was rushing towards him to pass him, and to it he struggled, his limbs already lethargic from chill. A protruding stick darted at him as though it were the fin of a shark, and with mighty effort he struck forward to miss it by a few inches.

Then he was at the 'island', and wisely ceased all movement save with his hands to grasp at a bough above the surface. The current swept his body against a submerged log and against the log he braced his body. Tom Pink's blue face was three yards from him.

'Can't you swim, Tom?' he called to the jockey, who was staring with eyes as glassy as the water.

'I can't swim – I can't swim,' Tom said with natural articulation.

'Well, you will have to do exactly what I tell you.

Do you understand?'

'What is it I'se got ter do? I'll do anythink to get outer this.'

'When I tell you to, you have got to let go that branch.'

'Let go. I daren't! I'll sink and drown.'

'You won't be able to hang on much longer. And very soon I'll be that numbed that when you are forced to let go I'll not be able to save myself. Wait! I'll see if I can get nearer to you.'

Cautiously Roy felt with his feet the exact position of the log against which the current held his body. Were there no snags between it and the bough to which Pink tenaciously held, he might reach the same bough, but if he missed it he would be swept past the man and then unable to render assistance if Tom maintained his hold.

'Let go, Tom. Do you hear? I'm with you.'

'I daren't. I can't swim. I'll drown,' Tom wailed. His voice rose to a scream. 'I'll drown – I'll drown. I'm slippin'! I can't hold on. I'm slippin'!'

Roy Masters risked much when he swung his body over the submerged trunk and let go his hold. Fortunately the few yards between Tom and him were clear. With two powerful strokes and one great kick off from the under-water log, he succeeded in reaching the jockey. And then, risking no further delay in fruitless urgings, he struck at Tom's hands clenched on the bough and cried at him to let loose.

The man screamed dreadfully whilst Roy beat his hands with one free fist. He screamed again when one hand was forced off the bough. Wildly that hand clutched for fresh hold, but numbness had paralysed the fingers. Again Tom screamed a moment before his remaining hand was forced off the bough, and down he sank.

It was, perhaps, fortunate for Roy that Tom Pink's body was too numb to enable him to struggle. When they came to the surface Roy managed to get behind the jockey and turn both Tom and himself on their backs.

To his vision was presented the grey sky. The clean rain, now almost stopped, caressed his face as with all the power of his legs he struck out for the bank. A seeming hour went by before tree tops began to obscure the sky, the branches of living trees growing along the bank, branches which slid by over him with unceasing velocity.

A snag grazed his back, and, offering a wild prayer that it was not many branched, he ceased movement to allow the current to sweep them over it. They were free. Tom began screaming again, yet was incapable of bodily movement. Another seeming hour loitered by, when a soft yielding substance rubbed against Roy's shoulders, and turning his head, he saw that it was the creek bank. And a dozen yards further down, swooping towards them, the gnarled out-stretching arms of a semi-submerged tree.

Where the devil was Jack? Why wasn't he there to render much needed help? A root projecting from the bank offered hold, gave it. Roy then was able to clutch Tom by one arm and glance up for a foothold.

'I'm coming,' he heard Jack shouting, as from a great distance.

And then it was he discovered that he had taken Tom Pink to the opposite bank, the bank nearest to Mount Lion. Jack and the horses were on the far bank in consequence.

'Hang on – I'm coming,' the stockman yelled again.

How could the fool come over when he couldn't swim?

There was no bridge.

What was he shouting about now? Was he gone mad, or was it at someone coming? No. There he was galloping up stream on a horse and leading two others on his offside. Now what? Jack and horses had vanished when they turned back from the creek. Yet Roy still could hear the man bellowing his hardest.

Tom Pink had not spoken since they had reached the bank. His body was limp. And Roy was now so numbed by the chill of this river of blood, that alone he could not have pulled his weight clear of the water.

The growing volume of Jack's shouting drew his attention to the opposite bank far up stream. There the bank was hardly a foot above the water level. Over that bank appeared the heads of three horses, the head of the solitary rider. Magically the bodies of the horses appeared, their outstretched legs, their flying hoofs. Ye Gods! They were jumping! Like three horses taking a steeple jump! Up and out. Then down with a mighty upflung spume of blood-flecked spray.

They were in - three horses and a man who couldn't swim. The fool - the reckless, dauntless fool. Three horses, heads in line, whilst above and behind them the shoulders and the head of a yelling devil who drove them.

'Kam up, *Skinflint*! Yo ho! I'm a-comin' there! Hang on! Now-now, *Flossie*, old tart. No drownding 'ere. There ain't time. Kam on, *Skinflint*. We're orl enjoying ourselves, so you got no argument. We're comin', Mister, we're comin'!'

As man and horses were swept by Roy and the dead, or unconscious jockey, the astounding stockman waved his battered felt hat as though he were a charioteer saluting his emperor, two thousand years ago. Deliberately he pulled back his horses to escape the tree below Roy, and, as many of its leaves still remained adhered to its twigs, the tree soon hid man and horses from the anxious owner of *Olary Boy*.

All that which followed appeared to Roy much as a disjointed dream. He remembered, afterwards, climbing up the bank, dragging Tom Pink with the assistance of the talkative Jack. Then he was astride a horse, a horse galloping madly across a gibber plain, on which the horizon was flung back to thirty and forty miles.

As he rode the horse without conscious feeling, so the demon of nightmare rode him. To Mount Lion - yes, to Mount Lion. A telegram - a telegram to Nat Sparks to stop him selling *Olary Boy*. Why sell *Olary Boy*? Stupid of him. He'd have to run in the Williamstown August Handicap and later at Caulfield in the Heatherlie Handicap. Then perhaps at Moonee Valley some time in September. Flemington - the Weight-for-Age would try *Olary Boy*, for he would be in good company. Of course! He might prove himself in that race and would then come on well at Caulfield. But not too well there, or he would carry too much later on. Then at Flemington again, and finally in the Melbourne Cup.

That was his race - *Olary Boy*'s. With careful and strict training, *Olary Boy* might win. Why not? What if he had a Roman nose? Didn't wall-eyed cattle dogs lick any other dog in a fight?

Houses! What's this? Mount Lion? Surely not. Couldn't be. A pub! A post office! The telegram! He could wire Nat Sparks from here:

'Excuse me. Write a telegram for me, please. My hands are too cold. Yes, an urgent wire, quick. What's that?

What do you say?'

'Sorry, sir, but all our wires are down,' the postmaster said - to add:

'Look out - catch him, Evans.'

7

The Doctor

It so happened that Mount Lion was fortunate in its bush nurse, and for Roy Masters it was fortunate, too, that she was home when Evans, the postal employee, went for her assistance. She ordered that he be put to bed at once, and, as there was no hospital at Mount Lion, it was into Mrs Bumpus's best bedroom that he was placed between blankets.

Beer was what Mr. Bumpus advised - hot beer heated with a red-hot poker, but Mrs. Bumpus named brandy, and in this she was supported by the nurse. So it was that Roy opened his eyes to find himself in a strange room with unfamiliar faces peering at him. His body was warm, when he had thought it never would be warm again, whilst the two women were comforting in their matronliness.

'What is the time?' was his first question. 'Where am I?' was his second. When informed that he was at Mount Lion and that it was half-past two, or thereabouts, he sighed resignedly over the sure sale of *Olary Boy* - and suddenly remembered Tom Pink and Jack, the stockman.

'You must send a car at once to Red Creek,' he said imperatively. 'I left a man there named Tom Pink in charge of a stockman called Jack. Pink was almost drowned in the creek, and when I left them, the stockman had managed to get a fire going, but Pink was in a bad way. You'll send that car off at once?'

'I'll send Bumpus,' decided Mrs. Bumpus.

'And get him to take some brandy with him. I'll pay all the expenses, of course.'

'There won't be any need to tell Bumpus to take brandy with him,' declared the publican's wife.

A few minutes later, Roy heard the hotel car move off. He was feeling fit enough to get up, but could not see his clothes. As there was no bell with which to summon service, he called. To Mrs. Bumpus, who came, he said: 'Bring my clothes, please. I will get up.'

'You'll stay where you are until Nurse comes to look at you again at five o'clock.'

As he had resigned himself to losing his horse, so did he resign himself to the fate dictated by this shrewd but kindly woman, who had so much practice in obtaining obedience from her husband that she had little difficulty in commanding obedience of other men. And, in any case, Roy Masters found the role of invalid by no means irksome. His body ached from the unaccustomed hard riding; the brandy given him had created a soothing lethargy which created the desire for sleep.

When he awoke it was dark and the room was illuminated by an oil lamp. Mrs. Bumpus answered his call, carrying a large tray of supper things.

'It will be a mercy if you don't all die of pneumonia,' she said, fussing about him and the tray at the same time. 'Tom Pink's pretty crook, but Fred is all right. An' you look all right, but in bed you stays till tomorrow.'

'Is Pink very ill?'

'Not so ill as Nurse thinks he's going to be.'

'No doctor here?'

'No. We 'ad one once but the drink got him.'

'Telegraphic communication restored yet?'

Mrs. Bumpus shook her head.

'Where is the nearest doctor?'

'There's one at Milparinka.'

'Then he must be sent for.'

'Milparinka's twenty-six miles from here. Mister - what is your name?'

'Masters. Tell your husband I would like to speak to him, please.'

Presently Mr. Bumpus entered.

'I understand that Pink is ill,' Roy said abruptly.

'He is so.'

'Well, send for or fetch the nearest doctor. I will pay all expenses.'

'No go. The telegraph is down, Mr. Masters. We can drive a car as far as Red Creek one road and for nine miles on the 'Parinka Road. Hard gibber country. The rain is gone and a car might get through to Bulka one way, 'Parinka the other tomorrow. Anyway, 'tain't no use worrying. Nurse is as good as any quack, but if Tom is worse tomorrow I could try for the 'Parinka doctor. An' the telegraph might be fixed tomorrow sometime.'

'Is Fred in bed, too?'

'No. They put 'im to bed and took orl 'is clothes away, but he got up and cum into the bar for a drink with a bed quilt round 'im. So we give 'im his clothes for decency's sake. But don't you go wearing no quilts about the place.'

'All right. Ask Fred to come and see me, will you?'

Fred's debut was delayed, and when he did announce himself it was to enter with a bulging hip pocket. His face had lost a little of its mahogany colour and gained a tint of red. Solemnly he withdrew from the hip pocket a bottle of whisky, and from each of his coat pockets a small tumbler.

'I've brought you a snifter,' he said after silently closing the door. 'They reckoned I was gonner get pew-monia. Just fancy a man getting pew-monia in a pub. 'Ow're you feelin'?'

'Fine. I want to get up, but they have taken away my clothes. No, thank you - I won't have a drink just now. Too soon after tea. How did you get on after I left you with Tom?'

Fred sat down on the bed with the bottle at his side and one of the glasses filled with raw whisky.

'Luck!' he exploded. 'After getting that fire alight I'm takin' a ticket in Tatts. Lemme see! Yes, that's right. You and me resusticates ole Tom Pink afore you gits away. Well, when I'd got that fire going proper there was flames risin' twelve feet high. I makes Tom off with 'is clothes, and I offs with mine, and while they're drying 'im and me are walking up and down in front of the blaze. Tom, 'e's being sick now and then – musta been the crick he swallowed – says he want to sit down, and we being like niggers at a corroboree. The rain was stoppin', and though the clothes was singed a bit, I got 'em dry. Ole Tom, 'e buck up presently, so I gits his clothes on 'im and lets 'im sit on a log I rolled near the fire. But 'e's mighty sick. Looks garstly. We could 'ave both done with a drink of tea.

'Tom begins to shiver, so I at 'im again, and walks 'im round, 'is feet coming about a yard be'ind 'is head. He still shivers, and us so close agin the fire that I got blisters on me arms. Then 'e gits 'ot and wants to tear 'is clothes off.'

Roy learned later that when their clothes were dry, Jack put his vest, shirt and coat over those garments worn by Pink, and that on the arrival of Bumpus he was naked from the waist up excepting his old felt hat. Continuing the quaint recital, Jack said:

'And then ole Bumpus arrived. 'Is car was one mass of mud, and the chained wheels looked like disc wheels. I says: "Did you bring any grog with you? Ole Tom is all in." "Too right," he says, and comes over to the fire with a cuppler bottles, a billy can and a tin of water - not Red Crick water.

'So we gits a full pint of stiff whisky down ole Tom's neck an' 'as a good snifter ourselves. Then we wrapped Tom in the blankets Mrs. Bumpus sent and sits 'im in the car like 'es was a stolen mummy, and orf we comes. I 'ope 'e ain't goona git too crook.'

'So do I. Is he very ill?'

'Seems like it,' Jack admitted, manipulating the bottle, to add solemnly: 'But I'm orl right. I took it in time. 'Ere's 'ow!'

'Who is with him?' Roy pressed.

'Mrs. Bumpus and Nurse,' Jack replied.

'Now, don't you get to worrying, Mister. Ole Tom's orle right. Nurse ain't never lost a case yet.'

Jack explained how Tom Pink, having been discharged by Mr. Smith for riding *Darling* to win, decided to ride to Bulka to seek racehorse work with Roy or Dick, having learned they owned horses. He set out from Mount Lion at daybreak. Arrived at Red Creek, so great his anxiety to secure employment, he had ridden his horse into the flood water, although unable to swim, with the result described.

'He must want work badly enough, to risk his life like that,' Roy said quietly.

'Too right, Mister,' Jack agreed fervently, as though he had not done the same thing - if with slightly more necessity. 'Ole Tom is a racin' man. It's in 'is blood. He'd 'ave been a champeen jockey if it weren't for the booze. He'd a' bin a champeen trainer, too, if it 'adn't bin for that. Know's more about 'orses than a vet an' can hardly write 'is name. An' straight, too. That's wot I like about ole Tom. It 'urt 'im to have to ride a dead 'un. That's why 'e trotted past the stand like 'e did. Well, I'll see you after, Mister. So long.'

The nurse visited Roy and pronounced him fit to get up in the morning. Pink, she thought, was in for a bout of pneumonia. Yes, they would try to get the doctor as quickly as possible; but he, Roy, was not to worry.

In the morning Pink was worse and Roy induced one of the storekeepers, who owned a more powerful car than Mr. Bumpus, to send it for the doctor at Milparinka. The driver was accompanied by two other men. They took with them a roll of netting, and several jacks and shorts lengths of squared timber with which to extract the car, if bogged.

The doctor arrived at sundown, and for the second time Tom Pink's life was saved.

And the following day Dick Cusack arrived in his single seater, the water in Red Creek having subsided as rapidly as it had risen, which is the way of many back country creeks. He brought with him Roy's luggage.

'We were getting a bit anxious about you,' he explained. 'The rider not returning to the Ten-mile night before last, the other man rode to Red Creek yesterday and reported that he found no sign either of you or his mate. The telephone wire was busted in a dozen places. Suppose we'll be getting down to Broken Hill tomorrow?'

'Better leave the start till the morning,' Roy agreed. 'Back in Vic, I'll have to get busy looking for a likely horse, and there will be precious little time.'

'Oh - I forgot to tell you about that, Roy. After you left I got a horse from Tindale and managed to get across to Moorabbin, where I wired your man, Sparks, not to sell *Olary Boy*. Waited for a reply, as the line, via Wilcannia, was all right. Sparks wired back O.K.'

'You rode to Moorabbin, Dick?'

'Yes, it was tough going, but I got there all right.' Dick replied casually, and omitted to tell how that terrific ride had cost two horses their lives.

8

Silly Little Fool

Roy parted from his friend, Dick Cusack, at Mildura after a slow and trying trip from Mount Lion, via Broken Hill. Of the two young men, Dick was the more pessimistic of winning the Cup with *Pieface*, and pessimism with him was an emphatic incongruity. Nevertheless, both had mapped out the races in which their respective horses would run; *Pieface* working slowly down to the metropolitan courses, where he would meet Roy's brown gelding at Caulfield early in September.

It has been said by many eminent divines that modern youth is given too much to worldly pleasures, a statement with a grain of truth, which is but a minute fraction of the whole. Like a great majority of young men, Roy was tremendously keen on his job, and he entered his office precisely one hour after his arrival at Spencer Street.

'Mr. Masters wishes to see you,' a clerk told him, and, knowing his father's passion for speed in business, he lost no time in reaching the elevator, which deposited him on the top floor of the huge Masters building in Collins Street.

The proprietor of one of Melbourne's big businesses was engaged when the son entered the plainly furnished office suite which looked out on to the roof garden. And possibly that garden was the explanation of why old Masters had his

49

office on the top and not on the ground floor.

'All right - we'll buy that stock at fourteen thousand, not a pound more,' Roy heard his father say to one of the managers whilst he stood before the high French windows overlooking the garden. 'So you're back.'

'Yes, got in this morning,' Roy replied, taking the chair opposite a square nugget of a man, whose bulldog appearance proved that his son took after his long deceased wife. 'I had quite a good fortnight.'

'Huh-hum! Couldn't afford a holiday when I was your age,' growled the old man, whose mental vitality and strength were unimpaired by his seventy years. Then, as though his mouth were a gun, he shot out: 'What are we paying you?'

'You know that you make me an allowance of two thousand a year,' Roy answered, smilingly.

'No allowance about it - wages. You've been worth it. Although doubtful, I accepted your report on those new silk looms and bought. They are turning out a good article. Your wages are raised by five hundred. Now - what did you think of Senor Alverey?'

'Highly polished, a little greasy, mentally, not physically. Why?'

'Greasy any way you like, but he can make money. The man who knows how to make money is a greater hero to me than Nelson, Gladstone or Milton. Must be going to stay in the country for a bit. I've just heard he's offered Kingsley six thousand pounds for *King's Lee*.'

'Oh!' exclaimed the startled Roy, 'That's a lot of money even for such a splendid race getter.'

'It is. It is, too, a bit of a mystery.'

'Dick Cusack and I both proposed to Diana Ross and we

were rejected.'

'Hug-hum! Silly little fool. But what's she got to do with Alverey buying a horse?'

Old Masters - we will name him as every one of his employees affectionately did - regarded his son with a stony face and with eyes which held a ghost of a twinkle.

Roy explained how Alverey had proposed to Diana, of the condition Diana had laid down to decide her choice, between Dick and himself, and how Alverey had been caught listening, whilst his friend and he discussed it.

'Hug-hum! You will have to look out for a good galloper. Get hold of the best trainer in Australia. I pay - as usual.'

'You won't pay in this instance, Dad,' Roy said with finality. 'I've got a possible; I've got a good trainer - and I am getting a good jockey.'

'You seem to be very fortunate,' Old Masters stated in tones quite free of sarcasm. 'Anyway, I'll keep my eye on Senor Alverey.'

He charged a well-worn and blackened pipe, reflected for a moment, and then said as though he discussed business:

'You're quite sure you love this girl?'

'Quite,' Roy replied steadily.

'Hug-hum. I didn't get married until I was past forty. Couldn't afford to. No credit to me, anyway - being poor at forty. You think Senor Alverey is in the running to win the Melbourne Cup and Diana with young Cusack and you?'

'Looks like it, Dad,' Roy hesitatingly agreed - to add, when on his feet: 'Well, I'll go, I have a lot of arrears of work to get through.'

'Hug-hum. Dine with me tonight, will you?'

'Righto. I'll see you at seven,' the smiling son said to the still stony father. But in Old Masters' eyes love lurked up to the instant he banged his desk for his secretary.

How like the old Dad, mused Roy, as he dropped down to the ground floor. Old Masters would have frowned at any extra expenditure incurred by Dick and him over this futile effort to win the Melbourne Cup. Such competition would be within their own circle; but with Senor Alverey, an outsider, coming into it, money would be no object when counted in the scales of chance.

The next week-end Roy paid a flying visit to his racing headquarters owned by Nat Sparks. He watched *Olary Boy* at work - and became almost as pessimistic as Dick was about *Pieface.*

'He's got it in him, Mr. Roy, if only we could unlimber his muscles,' Nat stated with conviction, whilst they watched the gelding gallop by them with a diminutive jockey on his back. He did the half-mile yesterday in fifty-four seconds, which isn't as good as I am sure he could do.'

'All right, we'll try him, Nat. You arranged his nominations for the Cups?'

'I did as soon as I got your blessed telegram from Milparinka. That was a good thought of mine to get you to sign 'em before you went. I'd have took it bad if we had parted with *Olary Boy.*'

'Well, I'll be getting back to town, Nat. Oh, by the way, other things being equal, that is if he lives through a bad bout of pneumonia. I want you to take on a jockey named Tom Pink. I've had good reports of him and wish to give him a chance.'

'He'll get it, Mr. Roy.'

Owner and trainer parted with the warm grip of

friendship, and Roy sped back to town, where a newspaper poster informed him that '£6000 buys *King's Lee.*'

So Alverey had purchased *King's Lee,* a champion galloper! Decidedly, he had paid for him. Still it made the odds no higher against *Pieface* and *Olary Boy,* who would have to contend against Australia's best in any case.

He wondered if Diana had extended to the Argentinian the same 'wee chance' offered to Dick and him, and the possibility of it hurt a little.

Olary Boy ran twelfth in the Second Division of the Kambrook Trial at Caulfield, although he merely carried eight stone seven. But he had a bad start, being last away at the barrier. Through Roy's mind a phrase repeated itself. 'A good little one will always beat a moderate big one.'

Dash it! *Olary Boy* was not a good little one.

On July the first, Nat Sparks wired: 'Tom Pink arrived. Still sick. Wife makes him wear a mask.'

Nat Sparks despatched another telegram ten days after the first: 'COME DOWN AS SOON AS CONVENIENT.'

TOM PINK

9

His Chance

When Roy reached Nat Sparks's house – a neat little villa flanked by stables and men's quarters, and the whole surrounded by a thousand acres of grassland – the trainer wasted no time before coming to the reason behind his second telegram.

'Look here, Mr. Roy, we'll have to get rid of this Tom Pink. During the first week he was here, when he was still a bit shaky after his illness, he was all right. I must say that he knows his business. He's a better vet, than I am, and suggested alterations to *Olary Boy*'s diet which already had made a difference. But for three days he's been blind drunk. He's upset my wife and he's upset my other boys.'

'Where is he now?'

'Over in his bunk,' Sparks replied angrily. 'I'll take you across.'

They found Tom Pink sitting on his bed playing a mournful tune on a mouth organ. Even the skin of his bald head was flushed, as was his face, with the effects of over-indulgence.

'Well, Tom? You seem to be going the pace,' Roy said cheerfully.

'I-I-I'se 'ad a break-out. Ooo are you?'

'I am Masters.'

Tom Pink's bleary eyes widened. The mouth organ slipped from his fingers to the floor. 'Oh!' he drawled slowly. With effort, his face indicating part shame, part mortification, he stood up to face the man who had paid all his expenses from Mount Lion and now was paying him to work. 'I-I-I ain't got nothing t-t-to say.'

'But I have,' Roy said, very much like his father would have done. 'Sit down, Nat - leave us for a few minutes, there's a good fellow.' And then when the trainer had gone: 'How drunk are you? Are you too drunk to understand what I am saying?'

'N-No, Mr. Masters.'

For a little space, Roy stared silently at the jockey. Then:

'In ordinary circumstances I would not think of mentioning it, but these are not ordinary circumstances. If it wasn't that I risked my life for you, you would have choked to death in that flood known as Red Creek. I rather fancy you owe me something.'

'T-t-too right, Mr. Masters. Gimme another chance. I-I-I'll go straight.'

'Now listen. When you're not on a horse, keep your face turned down,' Roy said brutally. 'It wasn't because you are Tom Pink that I saved your life. It made no difference to me if you were Jacky, the abo. I want you to work for me, and for that you won't owe me anything, because you will be well paid. But I pulled you out of a dickens of a mess by chance, and you now have the chance of assisting me out of a mess. Do you get that, or are you too fuddled to understand it?'

'Yes, I-I- g-g-get it all right,' Tom Pink lurched to his feet. He swayed in front of Roy, who was seated on a chair. 'I-I- Wait a mo,' he snarled, and, turning about, laid back the bed mattress, and revealed one unopened, and one partly filled, bottles of whisky. These he seized before staggering to the window.

'What are you going to do with the booze?' Roy asked calmly.

'Ch-ch-chuck it out. I'm through with it.'

'Give it to me. Waste not, want not.' The bottles changed hands. 'Now sit down again, and tell me what you think of *Olary Boy*.'

Tom attempted a pitiful smile, and clenched his great hands; and, because he spoke of a horse, it may have accounted for the fact that he stuttered seldom.

'He's orl right, Mr. Masters. 'E's a stayer. He wants buildin' up, though. 'E's got a funny disposition. A bloke he liked he'd do a lot for. H-he'd do a lot for me. Wot do you want 'im to do?'

'Win the Melbourne Cup,' Roy replied candidly.

He expected Tom Pink to throw back his head and shout with laughter. Instead, Pink said astoundingly:

'Let me train 'im and let me ride 'im, an' 'e's got a better chance than the average horse that'll start. Wot are you smilin' at? You don't seem to 'preciate *Olary Boy*. I'll bet you - I'll bet you a level tenner I sails 'im into a place.'

'You'd lose your tenner. At Flemington you'd get that drunk you wouldn't—'

'Ain't I just said I'd finished with the booze?'

'I suppose you have said that a thousand times.'

'I've never s-said it afore, 'cos I've never made up me mind afore. You gonna put me in charge of *Olary Boy*?'

Roy pondered.

'Gimme the chance, Mr. Masters. Me riding papers are

O.K. I ain't a registered trainer and don't need to be. I can work under Mr. Sparks. Let me stable and work *Olary Boy*, and 'im and me will get our chance to do somethink.'

Roy continued to ponder. Memory flooded his brain with pictures of this man sinking into a saddle, when his body lost its ugliness; of words spoken in praise by *Darling*'s owner; by Jack, the stockman; and just recently by Nat Sparks. He reached to the table for the glass, uncorked the used bottle, filled the glass with spirit. Then, with assumed cheerfulness, he said:

'Well, we'll have a drink on *Olary Boy*'s future success,' and leaned forward with the glass on offer.

Tom took the glass, held it up that he might look through the golden liquid, and slowly tilted the glass over the floor.

'I said, waste not, want not,' Roy stated.

'An' I said, to hell with the drink. Was you deaf, Mr. Masters?'

'I've a good mind, Tom, to give you your chance, and I will tell you something to prove how vital my decision is. I think it improbable - but if *Olary Boy* should win the Melbourne Cup I would receive something of greater value than the Cup and the stake money.'

'Wot's that?'

'The woman I love, Tom.'

'Well, I've b-b-been askin' for a chance, ain't I?'

'You may have it, I'll fix it with Sparks to let you have free rein with *Olary Boy*. You can ride him in the Williamstown August Handicap on the twenty-third of this month. If he goes well then, you can carry on with him.

'G-good! Now I know me onions.'

'I hope so, Tom. So long.'

His mind weighted by grave doubts of Tom Pink on more than one score, Roy drove back to town. The weather was fine and cold, and he ached to be able to go to Mount Kosciusko with Diana and her friends. Alverey would be there, of course. Trust Alverey to allow the grass to sprout under feet.

The succeeding weeks passed quickly. Nevertheless, business occupied most of his waking hours, and the old man at the top of the building often insisted his son knocking off at a reasonable time and accompanying him to his magnificent home to dine, for Roy kept a separate establishment.

He went out in the August Handicap, run over eleven furlongs, with Pink on top, wearing Roy's colours of Cambridge Blue and white hoops and black cap.

'See his legs, Mr. Roy,' urged Nat Sparks.

'They seem to be not so lumpy,' Roy said, his binoculars levelled at his horse going with easy freedom to the barrier.

'You picked a good un in Tom Pink.'

'Think so?' asked Roy pleasurable.

'Best man ever I've had, in spite of his stuttering. He lives with that horse. Sleeps with him, would eat with him if I allowed it. He's fined down *Olary Boy*'s legs. He takes the horse out on the roads sometimes, and after them trips *Olary Boy* eats like an elephant. He knows more about horses than I do - fact.'

'Get out, Nat.'

'All right. You'll believe it soon. They're off.'

Roy watched the blue shirt and white cap amidst the bunched colours. Saw how *Olary Boy* was squeezed out in what otherwise would have been a fair start. Although nearly last at the second furlong, he was recovering at the mile. At the three-quarter mile he had passed *Dickinson* and *Boy Blue*, and was overhauling *Captain*, who had started at six to one.

'What do think of him? What do think of him?' Nat Sparks kept repeating.

At the half-mile *Olary Boy* was well among the leaders. Roy's heart thumped with pride and excitement. Surely his horse would not win? No - no! There was *Captain* creeping up! Go on, Tom! Ride him - ride him! They're in the straight. Come on, *Olary Boy*! A - oh! Look out! Look out! Look out for the fellow in the green and white check shirt! Look out for him! Come on *Olary Boy*!'

10

The Stranger

Olary Boy finished fifth in the August Handicap at Williamstown, giving Roy much happiness, even though at one point in the race the gelding looked much like securing a place. The horse's effort earned him a paragraph in a newspaper on the following Monday, when the turf expert wrote:—

> '*Olary Boy*, who has never been considered seriously on the metropolitan courses, even by his connections, revealed running qualities not before suspected. On his back was a stranger to Victorian racing, one Tom Pink. Pink rode ably, and it was due to his ability that he lifted *Olary Boy* out of a jamb shortly after the start into fifth position at the post.'

Of many thousands of readers of the paragraph, Diana, perhaps, was the most pleased. She clipped the cutting and pasted it into an album in which she intended to record the careers of her friends' horses up to the Melbourne Cup. And of the paragraph writer's remarks, Tom Pink was the proudest, and the writer himself should have been proud, too, for Tom kept his cutting in an old race calendar and read it ten or twelve times each day.

Nat Sparks was quite truthful when he said that Tom Pink slept with the horse, and would have eaten with him if licence had been extended to that length. There occurred slight friction between the new jockey and the head stableman.

But the matters eased after a two hours' fight in which neither combatant gained a victory.

Twice a week Tom Pink took *Olary Boy* on a long afternoon saunter along the roads. From the moment they left Nat Sparks's property until the moment they arrived back, when on those excursions, the man kept up an incessant monologue with the horse. Had there been one to observe them he would never have admitted it was a monologue, because the actions of the horse almost proved it to be a dialogue.

'They takes yer out and they turns you round without seein' if you wants ter run or would sooner 'ave a shuteye,' Tom said without a stutter. 'When a 'uman being trains 'isself he can complain if 'e's got the tummy-ache, or feels tired, or suffers from stiffness. But a 'orse, 'e can't talk English, and only one 'uman being in one million can understand Horsey, which is your language.

'You're like my ole man. He 'ad plenty of muscle, plenty of bone. He liked 'is tucker and 'is beer–'specially 'is beer—but 'is long life was governed by the ole word 'sooner'. 'E would sooner sleep than work. 'E would sooner drink beer than work. In fac', 'e would sooner do anythink but work.

'An' that's 'ow you was, *Olary Boy*, till I come along fer you to tell me all about it. Now, here's where we dig up some of the roots you like. Only for 'eaven's sake don't go an' tell anyone our little secret.'

The ugly biped dismounted, leaving the reins over the ugly horse's neck. The road was long and straight and empty. By the side of the road, on the border of grass and shrubs and herbage, Tom slowly walked, his eyes searching the ground, an opened clasp-knife in his hand. The horse followed, gently nosing Tom's coat collar, and when the jockey suddenly fell to his knees, the horse stood with lowered head, his nose very close to the clasp-knife which was digging up a plant much like the salt-bush of the inlands. It was the long, slender root, which bled profusely where the knife had cut it, for which *Olary Boy* now exhibited intense passion.

'Lemme see! Yes - medium weight. One, ole Snozzler. I must gather a stack of these before September.'

Olary Boy greatly appreciated the root, for, having chewed and swallowed it, he turned back his upper lip, before begging for more. With the foliage of the plant he would have nothing to do.

Then on again proceeded man and horse for ten minutes, when a second halt was made to dig up and eat another root similar to the first. Three such roots did Tom give *Olary Boy* on Sundays and Wednesdays, roots the animal relished much more than the average horse likes sugar. The root supplied exactly what the animal's body lacked and craved for.

On their way home they came to a man seated on a gate. He was, as Tom saw, a member of that peculiar type found lounging around training quarters.

'Day!' this person said.

Tom Pink nodded, *Olary Boy* walked on. Then:

'Want to earn a fiver?' asked the man on the gate.

'Too right,' Tom snapped out, and wheeled the horse.

Having dismounted, and so coming face to face with the gate-sitter, he asked:

'W-w-well - w-w-what about it?'

Possessing no handkerchief, the man wiped his unshaven face with a coat sleeve.

'I'm wantin' a little information,' he said without annoyance, as though Tom had spluttered at him every day for six months.

'And you're g-g-givin' five quid fer it?'

The other nodded, preparatory to saying:

'Oo's this Tom Pink now ridin' for Sparks?'

'You're torkin' to 'im.'

'Oh! Is that *Olary Boy*?'

'Yus.'

'Comin' on abit, ain't he? I seen him gallop yesterday against a 'orse I thinks was *Linacre*. Was it *Linacre*?'

'Yus, I-i-it was.'

'What was *Olary's* time?'

'H-h-hand over your fiver.'

'Tell us first.'

'T-two minutes, f-f-fifteen seconds.'

'Cripes! 'E's slow.'

'Well - wot jer think 'e is? A r-r-racehorse? Come on - g-g-give us your fiver.'

A huge hand flashed towards the gate-sitter. Long ugly fingers gripped the man's coat lapels where they met. No longer was the man sitting on the gate. He was held semi-suspended in the air, his toes only resting on solid earth.

'F-f-fork out the fiver,' Tom Pink whispered.

'You lemme go,' the victim snarled. 'I was only bluffing. I ain't got no fiver.'

Tom Pink's left hand went on an exploration trip, and all it found was a ten shilling note, a letter, and a wad of newspaper cuttings. The newspaper cuttings he returned.

'Next t-time you speak t-ter m-me, I'll smack yer u-ug-ugly dial,' he said, and pushing the man back so violently that he crashed to the ground. Tom mounted *Olary Boy* and opened him out the remaining half mile to the gate giving entry to Nat's place.

The ten shillings he was sure he had earned by telling a fearful lie about *Olary Boy*'s recent running time. The letter interested him very much. It read:—

> 'Dear Bill,
>
> Your job is to watch *Olary Boy* and report often. If you can square the new man, Tom Pink, with the enclosed five pounds, do so. This is a little out of our line, but there's money in it - big money.
>
> Yours,
>
> Number Three of Four.'

Three of Four! What did that mean? And the gate-sitter had had five pounds with which to buy Tom and had spent it, probably on booze - and so came the double-cross! Tom Pink was very thoughtful all the evening.

Mr. Tindale

11

Will Do Well

On the afternoon of September 1, Diana Ross gave a tea party, to which a small select few were invited. From the Australian Alps she had gone for three weeks camping on the Barrier Reef. In Melbourne now but a few days, to her guardian's house in one of those quiet roads off the St. Kilda Beach were invited Senor Alverey, Roy and half-a-dozen others. Mr. Tindale did not wish to be present, having business to attend to, but consented at the last moment.

'Senor Alverey appears to have gone into the racing game with a big splash,' the squatter remarked whilst Diana and he awaited the arrival of the first guest. 'Spends six thousand on what must be admitted is a very fine horse, and now has prevailed on Newton to take charge of him.'

'Newton is a good trainer, isn't he?'

'Right on the top. He can ask what fees he likes and get them.'

'I wonder why Senor Alverey bought *King's Lee*. He once told me he was not at all keen on horses, guardie.'

'He seems to have been bitten hard, anyway. Perhaps, dear, it is because you are so keen on racing.'

'He is a most persistent man,' Diana sighed.

'You could do much worse than marry him. You could

marry him or anyone else, before you are twenty-five or six, which is quite early enough for a woman to bind herself with the chains of matrimony.'

'And yet I might be married within a month of the Melbourne Cup race,' Diana said with impish eyes, then went on to relate the facts of the almost impossible task she had set Roy Masters and Dick Cusack.

'You don't want me to marry, though, do you?'

Mr. Tindale's slate-blue eyes lost their steeliness when he replied tenderly:

'I have been your foster-father now for nine years. Have I ever given you cause to think that I could have been more paternally affectionate?'

'No, guardie, no, never.'

'As a matter of plain fact, were you to get married - and I suppose you will some day - I shall most certainly experience keen loss. A feeling which would be assured a good deal if I knew you to be married well. I don't mean by that, marrying money. Many men have huge fortunes and yet are nobodies. The kind of man I would like to see your husband would be he who had a certain big future - in diplomacy, for instance; Senor Alverey, a man of vision, able to transmute his dreams into reality.'

'Well, anyway, I have no wish to be married, guardie, so you may live in peace and content. I shall—There is our first visitor.'

Two girls floated in, in a quite unconventional manner, kissed Diana, and appeared about to kiss Mr. Tindale, when he hurriedly invited them nearer the fire, which he began to poke into a better blaze. The Argentinian millionaire came next, arriving in a magnificent coupe driven by a magnificent chauffeur. Roy Masters was the last to be announced.

'Hallo, Diana!' he greeted her, taking her hands. 'Enjoy your trip to the far north?'

'Splendid. I was so glad to see how well *Olary Boy* ran in the August Handicap at Williamstown.'

'Thank you. *Olary Boy*'s running was entirely due to his rider.'

'I think Smith was a fool to sack him,' the squatter put in.

'Agreed, Mr. Tindale. Pink will do well. Hallo, Alverey! Still on deck?'

'On deck? Ah - yees. You mean, going strong, in good health, eh? Yees I am, what you say, top hole.'

Alverey was smiling at Roy with his face, but not with his eyes, which retained the hardness that entered them when Roy arrived.

'Good! I am glad to see you Three of Four,' Roy said casually.

'Oh - you Australians. A new phrase, eh? Three of Four! These phrases, so numberless, are they to apply to the same thing?'

'Yes. Some of them are most expressive, are they not?'

A girl laughed, saying: 'How are you, Eve?'

Another girl answered, laughingly, 'Oh, Three of Four, thanks.'

Everyone laughed. Someone said of Roy that he always was most original. Alverey's face indicated no emotion whatever. It was a mask. Roy became less sure that the Argentinian knew something about the letter Tom Pink had taken from the gate-sitter.

And yet, as the afternoon wore on, Alverey cleverly eluded conversational contact with Roy. By no outward sign revealing to anyone that which he so subtly conveyed to Roy alone; which was decidedly not brotherly affection.

Yes, Senor Alverey had decided to run *King's Lee* for the two Cups. As everyone knew, *King's Lee* was a New Zealand bred horse imported to Australia as a two-year-old. He had come to the front as a three-year-old. Yes, after *King's Lee* won the famous Melbourne Cup, he would go to Argentina.

'He has it all mapped out,' Diana said softly to Roy when they were enjoying their first and only tete a tete that afternoon.

'By the way, did you offer him the wee chance you gave Dick and me?' he asked abruptly.

'No, Roy, of course not. Dick and you did not take me seriously, surely?'

'We did. And if either *Pieface* or *Olary Boy* wins that race we shall hold you to your terms.'

'Even if I didn't love the one who gained the Cup?' she asked him a little wistfully.

'You made the conditions, old thing. We didn't.'

'I know. And I shall abide by them.'

'Will you marry Alverey if he wins it?' was his next question.

'No,' she replied with conviction. 'Oh - we must mix in. You'll be at Caulfield, Saturday?'

'Yes - oh, yes. *Olary Boy* is running in the Heatherlie Handicap.'

'Is Tom Pink riding him?'

'Yes. You will see the difference Pink has made in the horse.'

'All right!' She furtively patted his arm and whispered 'Good luck', before rising and 'mixing in'.

Roy left Mr. Tindale's house experiencing pleasurable elation brought about by Diana's little pat on his arm and her whispered 'Good luck'. Despite everything, hope persisted in his heart, and he spent the days intervening between the tea party and the following Saturday with impatience.

The weather was brilliant, the race patrons flocking to Caulfield in their thousands. The smooth, velvety greenness of the lawns and the pine trees always reminded Diana of the Royal garden party she attended in England after her presentation at Court. At no other function, in no other circumstances, did she thrill as when she found herself on a splendid modern racecourse. Between the second and third races, Senor Alverey was her escort.

'No. I shall not bring *King's Lee* to Melbourne before October to run in the weight-for-age at Fla-Flemington, Meese Ross,' he informed her. 'Ah - that horse! A beautiful horse. He run so fine. In the Caulfield Cup will he win. The Melbourne Cup, too, he will bring me. And I - I, Meese Ross, to you will present those Cups.'

'Why?' she asked, calmly regarding his burning eyes. 'Not owning *King's Lee*, they would not be mine.'

'No? Then I have, what you say, copies made of them, of gold and jewels. I will lay these so precious cups at your feet, praying you to accept them, these cocktail shakers, for your side-board.'

Diana halted abruptly, and stared at the Argentinian. She could observe no mirth, no mockery, in his face, or in his eyes which blazed at her. One vertical line appeared between her brows. Was Alverey laughing at her, or had he spoken of cocktail shakers in ignorance? Surely not. He was far too polished a gentleman to offer a half-hidden give at her expense.

Quick to sense her changed mood, he tendered apology for anything he might have said not quite the thing, suspecting his reference to cocktail shakers and a sideboard, a fantastic allegory he had heard Dick Cusack use whilst he listened outside the window. Diana, however, dismissed his apology laughingly, and requested to be taken to the bird cage.

Here, as though behind the scenes of a theatre, the equine actors awaited their call, several kicking their stalls or tossing their heads, impatient of the delay in taking them into the limelight. A bay madam imagined herself queen of the Cannibal Islands whilst she walked about sedately with a small size in jockeys on her back.

Diana noted a well-dressed man raise his hat to them when he passed. To her, he was unknown, but Alverey knew him, for he returned the courtesy.

A quaint equine face looked at them from a stall which they passed. His upper lip was laid back over his nostrils in what was not a yawn, and then abruptly he returned to normal and whinnied, whinnied not at Diana and her escort, but at someone behind them.

Alverey swung round; Diana, a little less precipitately - to find Tom Pink regarding them with suspicious eyes.

'Theese - is he *Olary Boy*?' the Argentinian asked.

'Yus - 'e is. You b-b-backin' 'im?' Tom demanded, as though it were a sin to back any horse.

'I think not. I think he not win the Heatherlie Handicap. He – what you say? – not look a fast horse.'

'You're r-right, mister,' Tom said in spluttering agreement. ''E c-c-couldn't race an ant up a tree. I – 'Ere – stand aside! Gawd! Wot you done? What you done to *Olary*

Boy?' The jockey's eyes were blazing first at the Argentinian and then at Diana. With astonishment she noted how the pupils of his eyes contracted to little points of stabbing grey light. 'Hey, Mr. Sparks! Bill! Come quick! Come quick! Someone's doped *Olary Boy*. My Gawd! they've doped me ole cobber.'

Horrified by Tom's outrageous accusation, experiencing a strong desire to run before the hurrying crowd of men closed in on her, Diana turned round to look at the horse. But a few seconds since a healthy, intelligent lovable horse now revealed undoubted signs of physical distress.

Above the tumult she heard Tom Pink's voice screaming commands and curses. She seemed to be the centre of a mob of milling men. Alverey was lost to her on the outskirts of the throng. A man gripped her round the waist, and offered a path for them with his other fist. Arrest! Surely she was not being arrested? She had nothing to do with *Olary Boy* being doped. Then:

'It's all right, Diana,' spoke a well-known voice.

'Oh - oh, it's you, Roy. Oh, Roy, get me away, please!'

12

The Letter

'Why, you are all upset, Diana,' Roy said, becoming concerned. 'Steady now. Everything is all right.'

'But - but Roy, we didn't do it,' Diana protested, her eyes wide with horror.

'Do what?'

'Dope *Olary Boy*. We—'

'Of course you didn't dope *Olary Boy*. What an extraordinary thing to say!'

'But the jockey. Tom Pink, he shouted that we did.'

'Tom Pink did not refer to you or to Senor Alverey, rest assured,' Roy told her earnestly. 'I saw just what happened or rather just what didn't happen. I had come into the bird cage and espied you and Alverey standing facing *Olary Boy*. Tom Pink then was hurrying towards you. You turned round and spoke to him, and then suddenly he spun about and yelled out that *Olary Boy* had been doped. Even now we cannot be sure that the horse is doped.'

'Oh, but his is, Roy. He looked most peculiar. Now, you go back. I'll be all right. I'll be all right. I'll go along to the stand and hunt up guardie or one of the girls.'

'Sure you will be all right? I wouldn't leave you only I'm so anxious.'

'Quite sure,' Diana said, smiling bravely. 'You hurry back,

and then come and tell me just what has happened.'

'Very well - if you are feeling quite recovered. Are you?'

'Yes. But I was so frightened by all those men rushing towards us. Now go. I - I! Thank you for rescuing me.'

'Tush! I am mightily glad to have beaten Alverey to it,' Roy frankly said, before hurrying back to the bird cage entrance.

The lightning flash of rumour already had darted outward from the scene of the alleged doping, and Roy found difficulty in getting to the gate of the bird cage. Officials were keeping the people back, and to questions of: 'Is it *High Prince*?' and 'Is it this or that favourite horse?' replied invariably in the negative. Somehow Roy felt a little peeved that none asked if it were *Olary Boy*.

Of course, he was at once admitted. Over by *Olary Boy*'s stall there was but a small crowd gathered, the size of this crowd determined by three uniformed and several plain-clothes policemen, who were first questioning and then escorting to the entrance people who had no official business there.

'Make way, please,' Roy demanded authoritatively, which enabled him to reach the stall. Two vets, Nat Sparks and Tom Pink were working on the horse.

'Any hope of saving him, Nat?' Roy asked the trainer, clutching Sparks by the arm.

Sparks turned a rage-whitened face to his employer.

'Yes - with luck. I didn't think so a while back. Listen to Tom!'

'The d-d-dirty dogs. N-never mind, Snozzler. We'll get our own b-b-back on them d-dopin' swine. Come on - another gargle now. Just one m-more to ease them p-pains.'

The policeman standing by obviously thought as did everyone else, that the situation fully excused Tom Pink's lurid expletives, for he made no move even to remonstrate.

'Tom says there are a man and a woman in this,' Sparks growled. 'He saw them in front of the horse when he had left him only a minute.'

'They are above suspicion, Nat. The lady was Miss Ross, a very great friend of mine, and the man was Senor Alverey, the owner of *King's Lee*, and a millionaire.'

'Well, how did the horse get the dope? No one else was near him.'

'I don't know, Nat. But neither one of the two I have mentioned could possibly have done such a thing.'

'Well - it beats me. I could understand it better if *Olary Boy* was a top-notcher.'

'Remember the letter instructing that man to watch the horse, a letter signed by a mysterious Three of Four. There is something crook going on.'

'There is that. If we get *Olary Boy* over this he'll have to be guarded. He was comin' on well, and with a fair field might have got into a place.'

An hour later *Olary Boy* seemed to round a very nasty corner, and by the end of the day was able to get to the motor van which took him back to the quarters Nat Sparks shared with another trainer on the outskirts of Flemington.

After Roy had reported to the anxious Diana and her guardian, he ran into Senor Alverey.

'Ah - how is thee horse, Mistaire Masters?' inquired the Argentinian blandly.

'He will probably get over it,' Roy replied quietly. 'Are you aware that my jockey accused you of doping the animal?'

Senor Alverey's eyelids drooped. His voice, if anything became more bland.

'The - the mind of simpleecity hunts in the dark. Meese Ross and I stood admiring the horse. Nothing else. The horse - he was well. We turn our backs to heem to converse with the jockey and then when we turn to the horse again, heem very ill.'

Steadily Roy looked into the black eyes gleaming beneath semi-shut lids. For one second their eyes held in this steady stare as though they were duelling swordsmen.

'I did not think, and I am sure no one else does that you could possibly have done it,' Roy said quietly. 'Even if Miss Ross had not been with you, you would, as far as I can see, have no object in doping a second-rate horse. Everyone knows, of course, that *Olary Boy* is entered for the Melbourne Cup, but, again as everyone knows, he has a very poor chance against your horse, *King's Lee.*'

'I hope the beest horse wins, Mistaire Masters,' Alverey said, now smiling.

'I do, too. *King's Lee* running in the Hill Stakes at Rosehill, isn't he?'

'Yes, that is so. He will win.'

'Good. I'll put a tenner on him,' Roy said a little less coldly.

'Me! I put one thousand pounds on heem.'

'It is nice to be a millionaire. Au revoir.'

So these two parted, like two dogs unable to make their minds whether to fight or to be friends.

Both perturbed and mystified, Roy drove back to town, his sub-conscious entity controlling the car, his conscious mind constantly asking a question and demanding to this question a reply.

Who was behind the attack on *Olary Boy*? Now, more sure that his suspicions of Alverey were groundless, the elimination of the Argentinian increased the mystery. Diana had not given Alverey the 'wee chance', and, consequently, Roy became certain that the purchase of *King's Lee* was due to conceit. Having overheard the conversation between Dick and himself relative to the 'wee chance'. Alverey had got it into his head that if he should win the Melbourne Cup his siege to Diana's heart would be crowned with victory.

The possessor of such a horse as *King's Lee* would have no cause to fear his horse's defeat by either *Olary Boy* or *Pieface*. No - it was not logical to suspect Alverey.

Then who else was there to be suspected? Who was there interested enough in *Olary Boy* to fear his possible success in the immediate future or the distant future as represented by the Melbourne Cup? Dick Cusack? But how absurd. The very thought was an insult to his, Roy's, intelligence. To be sure, *Pieface* had done well in the Werribee Handicap early in June, and better still, at Bendigo in mid-August. But Dick! Good old sporting Dick! Perish the evil thought!

The paper that night announced the facts of the attack on *Olary Boy*, and when Roy met Old Masters at dinner his father's eyes were gleaming wickedly.

'Hum-hug! he grunted when Joyce, his butler-valet-slave put soup before him. 'Have you any mind about who doped the horse?'

'None, Dad.'

'Or who is behind the man who doped your horse?'

Roy shook his head.

'Joyce - the salt. Hum-hug! Think it was Alverey?' the old man pressed with astonishing freedom, before the butler of many parts.

'No. I can think of no one sufficiently concerned,' Roy replied with equal freedom, knowing how implicitly his father trusted Joyce, who had served him nearly thirty years. 'That there is someone out to do the horse an injury is obvious. Tom Pink, some time ago was bribed to impart information. He gave false information, and when the briber refused to part up, Tom went through his pockets. He purloined a letter which gave the briber instructions to try and bribe him. And the letter was signed most peculiarly - simply by the three words, Three of Four. I—'

'What the devil are you doing, Joyce?' roared Old Masters when the butler, then by the sideboard, clattered the plates.

'Sorry, sir. A plate slipped.'

'Well, remember I don't pay you to let plates slip. How did you say the letter was signed, Roy?'

'Three of Four. Just those three words,' Roy replied; and turned sharply round to observe Joyce. The butler then was midway between the sideboard and his end of the table. The man's face plainly indicated strain.

'You ill, Joyce?' Roy asked kindly.

'Er - no sir. Letting the plate fall upset me sir. I am seldom clumsy, sir.'

'Don't do it again. You might break a confounded plate and if you do the cost will be docked out of your wages,' Old Masters snapped. 'What's this? This New Zealand cod?'

'Yes, sir.'

'Hug-hum! I'll take your word for it it's not Port Phillip shark. Yes, it appears obvious that some gang or other is working against *Olary Boy*. Heard from Dick? Has he had any similar trouble?'

'He has not written so, and I heard from him last week,' Roy replied, and mentally cursed himself for permitting that vile suspicion to flare up again.

'Hum-hug! It's either him or Alverey. Alverey for choice. You are sure that letter was signed by Three of Four.'

'Of course; I have it here.'

Roy took the letter from his cigarette case and handed it to Joyce to take round to his father. He watched the butler lay the folded sheet on the right side of his father's plate. The old gentleman went on unconcernedly eating and only after he had finished the course did he raise his glasses on their black ribbon, affix them to his nose and take up the letter.

For what appeared to the curious Roy to be several seconds, his father studied that letter, with Joyce standing behind him, staring down at the letter over his shoulder, his eyes wide and most positively indicating terror.

'You are confoundedly impertinent, Joyce,' Old Masters said, in his business voice. 'I quite expect I shall have to sack you. Hum-hug!'

13

The Mysterious Mr. Leader

The next time Roy dined with Old Masters was on the Friday evening preceding the mid-September race fixture at Moonee Valley at which *Olary Boy* was to run in the Tullamarine Handicap, over a distance of one and one-quarter miles.

During dinner Joyce evidenced no nervousness when handling plates, or when actually serving, and his strange demeanour on that former occasion Roy put down to quite natural causes. Possibly the fellow was getting old; most certainly he was not overworked.

'How is that horse of yours going to run tomorrow, do you think?' Old Masters inquired, after the soup.

'It is difficult to prophesy, Dad. Nat says he has picked up wonderfully after that doping attack at Caulfield. It shook the horse a lot.'

'Salts of atropine they gave him, wasn't it?'

'Yes, but what agency was used to administer it remains a mystery. I see by tonight's paper that *King's Lee* is widely tipped to win the Hill Stakes at Rosehill.'

'He ought to find little difficulty in winning, according to what Leader told me this morning.'

'Ah - so you were discussing racing in business hours?' Roy said lightly.

Old Masters glared at his son.

'Horseracing was a minor subject. Of primary importance was Senor Alverey,' snapped the old man.

'Oh!'

'Yes. Leader was in Argentina a year. It is seldom that the son inherits the business acumen of the father, but young Alverey obviously does. Whether of set purpose or by accident, I don't know, but Leader informed me that Alverey found out several matters concerning Diana of which we were ignorant, and which may account for his determination to marry her.'

'Indeed!'

'Yes. Even though a man may be a millionaire, a woman whom he loves, in possession of about a quarter of a million pounds is preferable to the woman he loves possessing a bare patrimony.'

'I hardly follow you,' Roy said with knit brows.

'As I have just said. Alverey has discovered matters relating to Diana which we didn't know - until Leader told me.'

'Who is this Leader?'

'No matter - a business friend of mine,' Old Masters replied impatiently. 'Joyce, who supplied this meat?'

'Smith and Smith, sir,' replied the butler-valet-slave.

'Change the butcher, d'you hear? I don't expect any butcher to expect me to eat leather. Now, coming back to Diana and friend Alverey. Like me, Ross married late in life; in fact, later in life than I did. He had strange ideas about marriage; love, and all that. He foresaw that if Diana had possession of his fortune on her coming of age, she would be sought after by all the society adventurers in the world. And, knowing that the amount of that fortune is close upon a quarter of a million, I agree with him.'

'What!'

'A quarter of a million pounds, Roy. So what does old Ross do? He appointed his old friend, Tindale, and another friend named Harrison, as co-trustees over the money, giving them full control and with authority to act as he had secretly arranged with them.

'That knowledge anyone can gain. What Leader found out were the secret instructions given to Tindale and Harrison, which precisely was what Alverey learned.'

'What were they?' Roy asked when Old Masters abruptly ceased talking.

'That I am not going to divulge to you, son. You wouldn't thank me if I did. But the fool arrangement made by Ross is sufficient to induce even a man of Alverey's undoubted financial standing to go crooked.'

'In that case, I wish you had not told me as much.'

'It's done, Roy. What is it Joyce?'

'Perhaps later, sir.'

'What the devil do you mean?' Old Masters roared. 'What is it?'

Obviously reluctant, Joyce stammered:

'It is Mr. Leader, sir. He wishes to see you.'

'Where is he?'

'In the library, sir. He told me to tell you, sir, there is no hurry.'

'All the same if there were. I haven't finished my dinner yet. See that he has cigars and whisky. I will be with him presently.'

Without departing from his usual leisureliness, Old

Masters proceeded with, and completed, the really one good meal he permitted himself daily. He and his son discussed horses and their form; Mr. Tindale and his history where it interlocked with that of Charles Ross, deceased; and subjects of social importance, until their cigars finished, he said, rising:

'You will have to excuse me this evening, my boy. Leader and I have to discuss business. I hope *Olary Boy* will have luck tomorrow. You seem determined to stand by him and I think you are unwise not to snap up *Austral Pan* when he's on the market. He would give *King's Lee* a better race for the Cup than your horse.'

'I am sticking to *Olary Boy*,' Roy said firmly. 'To run *Austral Pan* would not be fair to Dick with his *Pieface*. As it is, *Pieface* and *Olary Boy* are in the same street. As you are pushing me out, I'll go now.'

'I hate to do it, Roy,' his father said regretfully.

Roy had travelled half-way to the city where he rented his flat when he remembered that he had left his overcoat at his father's house. The coat contained papers he would want early the next morning, and, because the evening was warm, he turned the car on St. Kilda Road and went back.

At the corner of the avenue in which was his father's house there was a solitary electric standard, and as he neared the standard so were three men walking towards it from the opposite direction. The light fell on their faces.

The middle man was Old Masters. On his left was Joyce, and on his right a tall man wearing a bowler hat and black overcoat.

Never had Roy known his father leave the house after dinner for any reason whatever. What was the valet doing with him? And was the third man the mysterious Mr. Leader?

14

A Good Trainer

About the time Roy Masters saw his father walking in the company of his valet, and a man he assumed to be a certain Mr. Leader, Tom Pink strolled across to the stable building, housing *Olary Boy* and several other horses.

His one hour's absence from the stables when darkness had set in was dictated by the trainer; emphatically not approved by the jockey-stable boy. Sparks, despite the dastardly attack on *Olary Boy*, found no logical reason why his horses should be especially guarded, and his reasoning was based on the assumption that *Olary Boy* had been doped in mistake for the favourite in the Heatherlie Handicap.

Since the transfer of Nat Sparks' race entrants from Bacchus Marsh to Flemington had been effected, Pink never left *Olary Boy*, save to eat his meals with the other employees and when supper time came round, he persuaded one of the boys to stay with *Olary Boy* during his absence.

At 10 o'clock this night, on the eve of the Mentone Handicap, September 24, Nat Sparks made his usual night inspection of his horses, and at the end of the inspection, the head stableman padlocked the main door before retiring with Sparks to their respective quarters, leaving Tom Pink to occupy a Coolgardie stretcher in a vacant stall next to *Olary Boy*.

That doping attack on *Olary Boy* was certainly a most peculiar affair. If it was deliberate, then what was the motive? Tom knew that, other than himself, no one considered *Olary Boy* fit to gain a place. Doping him, therefore, could not have been to assist some betting racket, and although the horse's form certainly had improved at the time of the attack, it was not so wonderfully improved that outside people would consider him seriously in their search for winners.

Why, he had only won two races the year before!

Anyway, it was time some of those horse dopers were brought to book. Look at the way they got at *Kambull* here at Moonee Valley and *Gunroom* at Caulfield, to say nothing of *Cevantes* at Kyneton. What kind of low swine must they be to poison horses? In the human scale, as low as the specimen who tosses poisoned baits over garden fences to poison people's dogs.

Lying there in the dark, undisturbed by jaws methodically munching fodder and the occasional stamp of a hoof on straw, Tom Pink's mind lazily pondered over several matters. He had been presented to Diana Ross, and was convinced that she was 'the finest tart' he had ever met. It appeared that Mr. Masters wanted to marry her and that she had promised to marry him if he won the Melbourne Cup with *Olary Boy*.

Very well - then *Olary Boy* would have to win, and that was all there was to it. One thing, he, Tom, had the proper sort of clay to make something worth while.

Old Nat Sparks was all right. He was a good trainer, but he had other horses to prepare for important races, and, therefore, couldn't devote to all those horses the time and study he could have devoted to any one of them. And because of him, Tom Pink, *Olary Boy* was going to be built up, and given an extra special chance to show what he could do.

A soft, and yet harsh sound awoke him at, his luminous watch revealed, ten minutes after two o'clock. The sound came from the main door, padlocked on the outside, all other doors being bolted on the inside. For perhaps five seconds Tom remained motionless on his bunk, his body half-raised, and supported by an elbow.

There was no mistaking that low, sinister sound. A well-oiled hacksaw was eating into the soft iron bar of the padlock fastening the door, and the hand working the hacksaw most decidedly was not the hand of Nat Sparks, or Mr. Masters, or Mr. Master's 'tart'.

While pulling on an old pair of elastic-sided boots, Tom Pink was as pleased as though he were about to welcome a rich and kindly uncle; for, in these most favourable of circumstances, he was placed in the position of the welcoming nephew.

Silently arrived before the door in his left hand – he always maintained his left arm was the strongest and most accurate – a mulga shillelagh, to gain possession of which nine out of every ten Irishmen would have picked a quarrel. It had knobs and spikes at the end of it which even the Molly Macguires would have banned.

'How's she going?' a whispered voice asked beyond the door.

'All right. I think I'm nearly through,' answered a second man. 'Step along, and see if One of Four is keeping proper watch.'

One of Four! So this was the gang who had ordered the gate-sitter to bribe him. Three of Four it had been who wrote the letter now in Mr. Masters's possession. Tom wondered if there were more than three men in league outside. Of course, the shillelagh would even things up a bit - especially the knobs and spikes on the end of it.

Yes, there was a lot to be paid back - quite a lot. Seven bad griping fits poor *Olary Boy* had. Fits which had forced agonised grunts out of him which had clamped his innards as though with red hot wire twitches. And more than seven hours of chills and sweats and faintness.

Tom Pink now had no doubt that the attack on *Olary Boy* was a mistake made by a man intending to get at another horse. And, too, he had now no doubt that the dopers were connected with the bird signing himself Three of Four, for outside somewhere on guard was another of that gang numbered so peculiarly One of Four.

'Ain't you through yet?' whispered a voice.

'Not quite.'

'Can you see what you're doing?'

'Of course not, you fool. But I can feel, can't I? Is One of Four all right?'

'Yes, 'e's seen nothink.'

For a short space the rasp of the hacksaw continued, finally to cease simultaneously with a sigh vented by the labourer.

'D'you know which stall *Olary Boy's* in?'

'No. We'll 'ave to use the flash.'

'All right. Fetch One of Four. He must stay here whilst we're both inside. You are sure there is none of the lads sleeping here?'

'Too right.'

Tom heard the severed bar of the lock raised and slipped

out of the U-bolt. He heard the heavy cross latch slowly and gently lifted and as gently allowed to settle at the bottom of the guide, whilst the door was pushed inward; and then, in the oblong of stark night, Tom saw the tall figure of a man wearing a felt hat, a new felt hat, for its outlines were clear, showing brim turned evenly upward and the crown neatly dented.

'Cum inside - just a cuppler feet,' Tom Pink mentally urged. 'Cum on, now, afore them other two get back.'

There is something in mental telepathy after all, because at this heart-felt invitation the man stepped inside the stable.

It is possible he might have seen Tom Pink standing against the wall on the latch side of the door had he not switched on his electric torch, the beam of which was carefully subdued by one thickness of a white handkerchief. Although sure he had made no movement, nor even breathed, Tom suddenly knew that the intruder had sensed his presence. He saw the man's body stiffen - but the man's sub-conscious instinct of self-preservation was not quick enough in muscular obedience to beat the shillelagh.

The sigh which issued from his lips was much less in sound volume than the impact of mulga against a skull. For a fraction of a second he swayed on his feet - to fall forward with stiffened knees and to be quickly dragged into the empty stall where was Tom's bunk.

Once again beside the door, the jockey waited for the next fly, or flies, to enter his web, confident that the first fly would remain stuck for quite a while.

Then there reached his ears the soft slithering of rubber protected boots and two seconds later, into the oblong of light fashioned by the door frame, entered the figures of a little man and a second man, who was neither so little nor so slim.

'I'm first,' Tom decided, referring mentally to the figure of wide and powerful aspect.

'Are you there, Two of Four?' demanded the powerful one.

'Cum inside - just a cuppler feet,' Tom mentally implored for the second time. Two of Four was sleeping the sleep of evil men, so which of these was One of Four, and what was the numbering of the other?

Receiving no answer from Two of Four, and neither of these men possessing flash lamp evidently, the sweating Tom Pink exerted his will-power without avail. It was useless repeatedly to dispatch the mental wireless invitation to 'Cum inside - just a cuppler feet', for now the shy guests were becoming suspicious.

'Where in hell is Two of Four?' demanded the stocky one. 'Sure he didn't tell you he was going skating?'

'Course not. Said he'd wait 'ere. Seems funny to me,' announces the other.

'Blast! And he's got the torch. Give me a match or two.'

'You can't strike a match 'ere,' countered the slim man. 'They'd see it from the quarters.'

'All right! Then you go inside and strike a light and see what you can see.'

'Me?'

'Yes. It's not going to be me. I don't like the look of things.'

'Oh, cum inside - cum inside a cuppler foot,' silently urged Tom Pink, his body balanced on his toes, his mouth drawn back into a wide leer.

'What shall we do? We gotta do something. Hey - you there. Two of Four?' the slim one called softly.

'Oh - give me those matches,' the other ordered sharply, and Tom heard the soft rattle of the box when it exchanged hands. Abruptly the powerful one stepped inside the doorway, striking a match at the same time.

Although he had never heard it, Tom Pink closely followed Admiral Lord Fisher's advice to naval gunners - Hit first, hit hard and keep on hitting.

15

They're Off!

The shillelagh did grievous work and Tom Pink was told by a police sergeant that he was lucky a serious charge had not to be laid against him. However, instead of accepting this admonition with the seriousness with which it was given, Tom screeched and stuttered in his best manner when giving to the police his private opinion about people who doped inoffensive horses. One of the men was well known to the police and wanted on another charge, whilst the other two duly served light sentences, because the heroin and hypodermic found on one of them had not been used.

But who employed them was not discovered.

Roy sat with Diana and Mr. Tindale in the Members' Stand watching *Black Tulip* win the brush steeplechase at Mentone the day after Tom Pink had dealt so harshly with three men. The girl was keyed to concert pitch because, against her guardian's advice, she had backed *Black Tulip* to win, and home he came in with a four lengths lead.

'I am going along to draw my money,' she said gaily to Roy, who, although he had lost his stake on a grey gelding who had crashed at one of the jumps, was as pleased almost as was Diana at *Black Tulip*'s performance.

'I will escort you, Diana - that is, if I may,' Mr. Tindale offered, his eyes twinkling.

'You may, guardie. Roy is aching to dash away to see *Olary Boy* off in the Mentone Handicap. Roy, I shall be in this same place waiting for you in twenty minutes. I want you to be with me so that you can describe the race. You will be here?'

'Your Majesty has but to command,' Roy assented with assumed gravity.

Down in the saddling paddock he found *Olary Boy* being walked around by Tom Pink, the race being devoted to apprentice riders, and a lad named Hurley being appointed to carry Roy's colours.

'I suppose, Tom, you are a little disappointed that you can't take out *Olary Boy* today?' Roy said, when looking up at Pink and walking beside the horse. Pink nodded, before whispering confidentially:

'If young Hurley remembers to ride 'im as I've told 'm 'ow to ride 'im, *Olary Boy* won't disgrace us. Any'ow, seven four ain't much for 'im to carry, an' I would have 'ad to sweat a lot to get down to that. Wot do you think of 'im, sir?'

'Who, Hurley?'

'No - the ole feller,' Pink replied, affectionately, patting the horse's shoulder. ''E's cum on well after the doping. G-good job we seen the horse when we did.'

'I am beginning to think, Tom, that you know a lot about a horse,' Roy said quietly. 'Just between ourselves, if you win the Melbourne Cup on him, I am going to make you a present of two thousand pounds.'

'You'll be doing no such thing, Mr. Masters,' Pink said earnestly. 'If me and ole Snozzler gets the Cup then you and me are quits over Red Crick. I'm then free of our contract about the booze. By that time I'll 'ave saved a decent cheque, and as ole Jack - you remember the bloke 'oo pulled us both out of Red Crick – as ole Jack Barnett is coming down, me and 'im is gonna 'ave a drink for ole time's sake.'

'By that time, Tom, I hope you will have realised the stupidity of doing anything of the sort. You keep sober and make your mark as a trainer.'

The warning bell for horses engaged in the Tullamarine Handicap sounded and Nat Sparks hurried up to them.

'Come on, Tom. Time. You coming to the mounting yard, Mr. Masters?'

'No, Nat. I am due in the Members' Stand. Good luck, old boy,' Roy added when he patted the horse before it was led away.

'I was hoping to be here before you,' he told Diana upon joining her.

'I slipped away from guardie when a friend engaged him in conversation, Roy. I wanted to have a little tete a tete with you.'

'Oh!'

She noted his brown eyes searching her face.

'Yes, I saw Dick yesterday. He made a rush trip to town about his wool. Met him quite by accident in Collins Street. So I made him take me to tea. Why didn't you tell me about Senor Alverey listening on the verandah whilst you and Dick discussed my silly wee chance?'

'Did Dick tell you about that?'

'I got it out of him with difficulty. Why did you keep it from me?'

'I did not think it of sufficient importance to bother you with it,' he said. 'Dick closed the matter with an upper cut.'

'Did - did he strike him?'

'Something like that. Look! There goes *Olary Boy*. And

there's Tom Pink down near the judges' box wringing his hands with anxiety.'

'And because Senor Alverey learned of the wee chance I gave Dick and you, he bought a champion with which to block either of you winning the Cup. Am I not right?'

'Looks like it Diana.'

'And it looks, too, as though he is trying to make certain sure that *Olary Boy* will be no danger to *King's Lee*.'

'Diana, you must not say that,' Roy said seriously.

'Well, I think it. Who else would have any reason to - to, well, you know.'

'Funny Dick never dug me up, Diana.'

'Not at all. He arrived in town yesterday morning and left again last night. I actually think he was annoyed with me because I made him take me to afternoon tea.'

'They're a long time getting away,' complained Roy, examining the horses at the barrier through his glasses. He felt a little hurt that Dick had not wired him the fact of his visit; and, too, that absurd suspicion would intrude. After all was said and done, Alverey had nothing to fear from *Olary Boy*.

'They're off,' he cried, and promptly forgot everything but the race in progress.

'*Olary Boy* got away well,' he went on. 'He's in the middle of the field, right behind *Master Vorst*. He's losing ground a bit. That's right Hurley, lad! Save him - save him. They're at the mile - *Radiant* in the lead, followed by *Gadfly*, then *Captain* and *Earl's Daughter* neck and neck. Then *Master Vorst* – There's a horse right on his tail – looks like *Nazi*. Yes, it's *Nazi*. He's creeping up beside *Olary Boy*—. He's coming along well. *Olary Boy* - Plenty of time, Hurley. Don't push him yet.

They're nearing the home turn. One - two - three - four - six - *Olary Boy* is seventh and keeping the pace well. Here they come along the straight.'

The gathering excitement of the crowd broke into a hum, rising quickly with a roar, unintelligible because it voiced the names of several horses and was filled with encomium for those several horses.

It was a good race, well run, the leaders almost abreast. *Nazi* won by a head, placing *Captain* second. And in the final burst, *Olary Boy* drew away from *Radiant* and gained third place.

'Oh Roy! Roy! How splendid!' Diana cried, on her feet, her face flushed into loveliness, her hands clapping.

'My word, he ran well, didn't he?'

'Oh, he did - he did! Did you expect it?'

'I did not, but I hoped it. Come along! Let's hurry down and welcome him in.'

A girl called out to Diana, but she did not hear her, so eager was she to reach the incoming horses. The course stewards were waiting in their huntsmen's scarlet to bring in the placed horses. Diana's eyes were shining, her mouth slightly parted, and her beauty made Roy catch his breath. It was the greatest minute ever he had lived.

Up went the numbers - two - eleven - fourteen. There was no mistake. His Roman nosed *Olary Boy* was placed third. Young Hurley smiled proudly at Nat Sparks, who held the horse whilst the lad dismounted, then to unsaddle and make his way to the weighing-in room.

Diana, Roy, and Tom Pink all met *Olary Boy* as Nat led him into the saddling paddock.

'He ran well, didn't he?' the gratified trainer called out

whilst yet there was distance between them.

They crowded round the horse.

'He's hardly damp, Nat,' Roy exclaimed, a trace of exultation in his voice.

Diana stood still. She said nothing. She was astonished by the ecstatic expression on Tom Pink's weather-beaten face. He threw an arm over and round *Olary Boy*'s neck. And *Olary Boy* affectionately rubbed his cheek against Tom's body.

'You old Snozzler! You damned ole Snozzler!' Tom said, oblivious to the presence of a lady.

16

Taken For A Ride

Olary Boy's performance in the Mentone Handicap gained for him serious attention by the sporting writers. One expert wrote: 'This ugly four-year-old gelding will bear watching,' while another opinion was expressed thus: 'A potential star in the racing firmament is *Olary Boy,* who, although his record is a poor one, shows great promise this spring by the rapid manner his form is improving. Entered for both Cups, Mr. Roy Masters' brown gelding may produce a surprise.'

After the determined attempt to get at *Olary Boy,* Nat Sparks took no further risks with him, finally being induced by Tom Pink to arrange a most efficient guard. While track work proceeded, Sparks even more frequently consulted the jockey.

King's Lee won the A. J. C. Derby, carrying seven stone seven. And a week later, at Wodonga, Dick Cusack's *Pieface* revealed unmistakable evidence of doping.

With indignation surging through him, yet lashed by self-contempt for his suspicion of his friend, Roy Masters read several times the account which appeared in the press the following Monday:

'Before the Wodonga Handicap Pieface began to perspire freely, and his conduct became so bad after the race that he was sent home by motor-float. When his trainer returned home after the races, the gelding's eyes had dilated to an alarming degree, and his mouth was as dry as tinder. He looked like a horse which had run 100 miles. He was restless and whimpered throughout Saturday night, and refused food. Up to a late hour last night he was slowly recovering.'

Accepting Roy's advice, Dick scratched *Pieface* in another country race and had him transferred to Nat Sparks' stables to keep company with *Olary Boy*. He did not run in the October Stakes (weight-for-age) at Flemington, but Roy's horse did, and despite the fact that *Olary Boy* found himself in superior company, he satisfied even Tom Pink by running fifth.

'He c-c-could 'ave done better, but I d-d-didn't ride 'im as I could 'ave rid 'im,' Tom explained to Roy when the latter visited *Olary Boy* one Sunday afternoon.

'Why was that?' Roy asked. 'Did you ride to Nat's instructions?'

'You w-w-wants *Olary Boy* to win the Melbourne Cup, don't you? All right, I d-d-don't aim to bring old Snozzler to top form one day b-b-before that race. 'Orses is like humans in training. They g-g-gets to a certain pitch, and th-th-then goes stale. We'll give 'im a solid race on the first day at Caulfield, an' again in the Caulfield Cup, an' for the Melbourne 'e'll be as fit as any of 'em.'

In the Herbert Power Handicap, *Olary Boy* gained third place, losing by only half a neck to *Captain* for second place. Dick's horse, *Pieface*, came home among the ruck.

In the Caulfield Cup, won by *King's Lee*, *Pieface* came in ahead of *Olary Boy*, the last-named taking sixth place, and this was no disgrace to the pride of Tom Pink's heart, for early in the race *Olary Boy* almost came to ground over the fallen *Black Princess.*

Olary Boy went out in the Hotham Handicap at 20 to 1, whilst there was no money on *Pieface*, who was quoted at 100 to 1. But *Olary Boy*, gaining second place, swung into public favour for the Melbourne Cup, ruling at 5 to 1 on the day before the race.

And on this day the gang behind the attacks on Roy's horse and *Pieface* made a desperate move. At nine o'clock at night, in a heavy rain-storm, a big enclosed car pulled up outside the training quarters occupied by Nat Sparks, and a man presented him with a letter which read:—

'51B Spring Street,

'Dear Nat,

As I shall be delayed tomorrow in reaching the course through pressure of business, please send Tom Pink to me in company of the bearer. The points I wish to discuss with him are important. Do not let him delay.

Yours,

Roy Masters.'

Asking the man to wait, Nat Sparks crossed to the stables and there read aloud Roy's letter.

'A-all right, I'll change me coat, get me oiler, and 'op away,' Tom agreed instantly.

'I can't think what Mr. Roy wants to talk to you about at this time of night,' Nat said.

'N-nor me, Nat. Still, orders is orders. I'll see you w-when I cum back. Hooroo.'

On joining the waiting man, Tom said: 'G-good n-night!' to which the other replied gruffly. 'Same to you.' At the car the door was opened and he was invited to enter the tonneau. There he discovered a man occupying the far end of the seat, he taking a middle position with his conductor on his right. At once the car slid away.

'G-gonna be fine for the Cup?' Tom cheerfully inquired.

'Hope so,' replied the man on his right. 'Care about a drink?'

'Yes, I c-cares a lot, but I ain't touching the booze t-till t-tomorrow night.'

'Frightened you'll go off the loose end?' came the sneered question.

'I am,' Tom announced candidly.

'One drink'll do you no harm,' suggested the man on Tom's left-hand.

'N-n-nope? Well - I'm d-decidin'.'

They had covered half the distance to the city when the engine began to stutter very much like Tom Pink. He could hear the driver swearing, and a few seconds later the car was pulled to the side of the street and stopped.

'What's the matter?' demanded one of Tom's companions.

'Don't know,' growled the driver. 'Might be water in the carburettor.'

'Well, you'd better hurry up and know. Mr. Masters wants Mr. Pink here quick.'

'Take a taxi. There's one on the other corner. I've always had trouble with the ignition of this bus.'

'A man ought to take an axe to it,' opined the one who had offered the drink. 'Come on. We'll grab that taxi.'

Tom was led across the road to a private taxi, whose driver was instructed to deposit them at 51B Spring Street.

When they moved off, Tom again sitting between the two men on the rear seat, he noted the driver of the other car walking rapidly away. And the direction he took was not towards the garage less than fifty yards distant.

At high speed the journey to the city was continued, several turns being taken. When they came into the lights of Spencer Street, Tom noticed that both his companions were slouched down into their respective corners, their trilby hats set forward over their eyes.

The driver's hat, he noticed, was comparatively new. The upturned brim was even. The man's prominent ears sharply reminded him of someone, but not until they reached William Street did the groping fingers of his mind produce the original.

The driver was the slim man who for a few seconds had been silhouetted beside a shorter and more powerful man in the oblong made by an open stable door.

Tom's heart missed two beats, and a coldness rose up his legs from his feet. He was in strange company, if the driver indeed was the man who had served a sentence of a month for breaking into Nat's stables.

'Hey, you, give us a gasper,' the jockey called loudly.

The driver, taken off his guard, partly turned his head, and in profile Tom became quite sure. Was he being taken for a ride? The chilling prospect banished his stutter.

'I gotta yell 'cos you blokes are so silent,' he said, turning to the man on his right. 'Anyone would think we was goin' to a funeral.'

The man was sitting with his arms folded, but the right hand was slipped under the left armpit.

'Yes, it's much like going to a funeral, isn't it? A cigarette?

Certainly,' And whilst he offered Tom his case, he chuckled at the jockey's little joke.

They crossed Queen Street.

'Give us a match,' Tom demanded of the second man, and this man sat with his hands in the pockets of his raincoat. He produced a box of matches with his left hand.

'Pull up, driver, I want to buy some gaspers.'

'Can't buy cigarettes this time of night,' pointed out the driver - without turning his head.

'Well, pull up, anyway. Do you hear?'

'We have to take you to Mr. Masters as quickly as possible,' the right hand man said levelly.

They were passing Elizabeth Street. It was almost as light as day, despite the falling rain.

Tom learned forward to tap the driver's shoulder.

'Don't worry him,' drawled his left companion. His companion on his right lowered swiftly the blind on that side of the car. That he was actually being 'taken for a ride' Tom was now sure.

He began to laugh just as they reached the Swanston Street intersection, and were stopped by the red traffic light. His laughter was a high-pitched scream of mirth. 'Fancy taking me for a ride!' he yelled. 'Ha-ha-ha! Reminds me of ole Noo York, where they puts 'em on the spot or takes 'em for a ride.'

'Shut up,' hissed his left hand neighbour. 'Shut up - d'you hear? If you don't stop it, I'll bash you.'

People waiting to cross the street stared curiously in at Tom, who now was quiet. The other blind was lowered. The red traffic light gave place to the amber light. The driver let out the clutch, and they began to glide across Swanston

Street. In complete shadow, Tom sat bolt upright between two men, who watched him like a pair of cats. A quick glance revealed their gleaming eyes beneath their hat brims.

With his heels hard against the bottom of the seat, Tom lunged forward, his arm straightening his hands slipping by each side of the driver's head, then to circle round the man's throat.

His companions grabbed him, but were not quick enough. The driver vented a piercing shriek when Tom's teeth closed on his right ear. One of the men behind him raised his reversed pistol in order to bring its butt down on Tom's head, but in that second the car, which had become uncontrollable when the driver's hands left the wheel, crashed into a stationary Spencer Street train.

'Get!' shouted the man with the reversed pistol, in a split second refraining from bringing it down on Tom's skull. They flung open the doors, and ran like dodging hares through the crowd.

When the police reached the wrecked car, they discovered Tom chewing the driver's other ear.

17

The Parade

The annual Cup pilgrimage to Melbourne had taken place; sailors from the fleet; politicians from Canberra, and every State capital; sportsmen from every town and city in the Commonwealth; boundary-riding stockmen, truck drivers and cooks from all over outer and central Australia, including Jack Barnett, who had swum three horses across Red Creek.

The only man who was not infected by the racing carnival spirit was he whose both ears were badly damaged.

Within half an hour of Tom Pink's arrival at the City watch-house, Roy had been located at his Club and had explained matters as far as he knew them. Of course, the letter to Nat Sparks was a clever forgery, and it was agreed that it had been determined by these unknown men either to abduct the jockey to prevent him riding *Olary Boy*, or, as Tom had surmised, they were taking him for a ride, in the American fashion.

All Australia was at Flemington on the first Tuesday in November. The Flat was a curved block of humanity. The entire Hill was hidden by the thousands there; whilst the lawns before the Members' and the Grandstands were the parade grounds of fashion.

After the rain, this veritable garden of a racecourse, with

its blooming roses, its beds of flowers and the white-painted railings gleamed with vivid hues, in rivalry with the tiny white puff-clouds dotting the brilliant blue sky.

Among all that huge multitude there could have been few people less interested in the races preceding the Melbourne Cup than Nat Sparks and Tom Pink, Diana Ross and Roy and Dick, who were with *Olary Boy* in the saddling paddock.

'L-look at 'im - look at ole S-s-Snozzler,' Tom implored the small group with him. *Olary Boy* was being quietly walked about in charge of a boy, and accompanying boy and horse were two tall men, who might have been bankers, but who were detectives. Every time *Olary Boy* walked from the group, he repeatedly turned his ugly head to look back.

'I believe he is looking for you, Mr. Pink,' Diana said laughingly.

'Too right, Miss Ross. Anyone w-w-would think I was 'is s-s-sweet'eart, w-wouldn't they?'

'Well, you are aren't you?'

'I-I don't know about b-being s-sweet'earts, Miss, b-but me an' 'im is good cobbers.'

'Another twenty-five minutes,' Nat murmured, watch in hand. 'By gum! I'll be glad when it's over.'

'Why the anxiety, Nat?'

'Why the anxiety?' the trainer repented. 'Ain't the authorities guardin' royalty mighty glad when their journey is ended, and the Kings and Queens safely locked up in their castles? I've been imagining fellows taking pot shots at those two horses with long-range rifles, and aeroplanes suddenly appearing to drop bombs on 'em. They're not safe even here.'

'We cannot do anything more,' Roy said, thoughtfully. '*Pieface* is looking well today.'

'They watched Dick's bay gelding brought out to follow *Olary Boy*.

'He won't be last, will *Pieface*,' was the trainer's opinion.

'And he won't be first,' Dick maintained, with a cheerful grin.

'Might.'

'Might not.'

A bell rang.

'Righto! Our number's up,' announced Nat with obvious relief. Tom Pink and Hurley hurried away to the jockey's room. Horses were moving out of the small saddling paddock and in their turn went *Olary Boy* and *Pieface* guarded by the detectives, Roy and Nat Sparks with all his available boys.

Their path lay across an open space from the saddling paddock to the end of the lane at that end of the Members' Stand, a path edged by packed people. In the lane which ran the whole length of the Members' Stand people crowded thick to watch the famous Melbourne Cup runners pass along to the mounting yard.

'There's *Captain*!' 'Here comes *Black Tulip*!' '*Olary Boy* - ugly isn't he?' '*Wayside Belle*.' 'Ah - *King's Lee*.' '*King's Lee* - I only got evens!' 'What's *Olary Boy*?' 'Oh - he's ten to one.'

So the scraps of comment which reached the escort attached to *Olary Boy* and his stablemate while they passed the crowd among which might lurk a sinister enemy.

'D—s! They're guarding *Pieface* and *Olary Boy*,' Roy heard a man tell a woman. '*Pieface*, what's the betting on him?' 'Dunno exactly. About 33/1 I should think.' '*King's Lee* - ain't he a hum-dinger?'

Near the mounting yard the band was playing a lively air.

People were swarming up into the vast stands like ants running up trees before the coming of a flood. Beyond, dimmed by the great building and the low hum of the crowd, there came the faint murmur of hoarse voices shouting the odds.

Tom Pink and Hurley came out of the jockey's room carrying whips. The detectives hovered near the gate leading out of the yard.

'Ride your best, Hurley?' Dick said softly when *Pieface*'s jockey was about to mount.

Hurley nodded, and smiled faintly, every nerve in him tense and vibrant.

'Don't you w-w-worry, Mr. Roy. M-me an' ole s-Snozzler gonna do our stuff.'

'That's right, Tom,' Roy agreed. 'Whatever the result, I'll know you will have done your damnedest.'

'You keep your eye on *Nazi*, Tom,' Nat whispered. 'I'd only be a fool to tell you how to ride *Olary Boy*, but I'm tellin' you to keep your eyes on *Nazi*'s jockey.'

'Righto, N-Nat. Well, hooroo,' And from *Olary Boy*'s back Tom Pink winked openly at owner and trainer and waved his hand to Diana standing outside the mounting yard waiting for Roy and Dick.

They glimpsed Alverey near the fidgeting *King's Lee*, and then were outside, hurrying off with Diana to get a good position in the Members' Stand from which to view the race.

18

21 Starters

Flushed and out of breath, the girl, with her escort, turned, when in the stand, to view the horses passing along the second lane to the entry to the course. There was *Pieface* carrying Dick's colours of red and white stripes and the red cap. Hullo! He was a little frisky or, perhaps, frightened! Her gaze came back to follow *Olary Boy*, Pink on top, riding as light as a feather. With all her heart she hoped *Olary Boy* would win – for Roy's sake, for Tom Pink's sake – for the sake of Dick Cusack's wagered thousand pounds.

Dear, loyal old Dick! It seemed almost that he wanted *Olary Boy* to win and so give his friend. . . There was *Olary Boy* prancing in the lane, awakened at last from his calm lethargy, apparently. Now he was trotting smartly towards the barrier. And there was her guardian coming towards the Members' Stand after having watched the horses pass along that second lane.

What a beauty! What a horse was *King's Lee* easily cantering down the course to the barrier! And *Black Tulip*! A jet-black, beautiful mare, full of life! More life than *Olary Boy* seemed to have in him. He might have been trotting out to a day's stock work for all the effect the colours and the massed people had on him.

Of nearly eighty horses nominated for the Melbourne

Cup early in June, only twenty-one arrived at the starting barrier.

Dingo Lad was given inside position, *Black Tulip* the outer, whilst *Olary Boy* and *Pieface* occupied respectively fifth and eleventh places. After his little flare-up in the lane, *Olary Boy* was behaving well, taking an intelligent, if bored, interest in *Black Princess*, who was electric with nervous excitement. The horses were on their toes, several of them already streaked with snowy lather.

A short delay, two fruitless line-ups:—then AWAY!

Tom Pink was experiencing no physical sensation, no feeling whatsoever. To him it appeared that he was just a mind poised above and behind *Olary Boy*'s head - a mind governed solely by one idea: to gain a place and keep it until near the end. But not the first place. As twenty other horses were pitted against *Olary Boy*, so were twenty other brains pitted against his brain.

Trained to face just such a barrier as this, *Olary Boy* bounded forward a split second before his rider's command reached him. In the comparative stillness of that part of the course, the twenty-one human contestants heard above the thudding hoofs the throbbing mighty voice announcing the start.

Twenty-one equine thoroughbreds, trained to the minute, each a poem of action, each a picture of wonderful beauty, almost in line abreast, running over a green ribbon that sharply divided great areas of colour-specked grey masses of people; massed people strangely silent after that first throbbing note; tens upon tens of thousands of minds, even as Tom Pink was a mind, incapable now of physical feeling, but shot through and through with flashes of spiritual ecstasy.

And with the fading, the vanishing of physical feeling, so the utter banishment in the sense of time. Time was not - and men were gods.

'Now, now, *Olary Boy*! Don't you make the pace for *Captain*. 'E thinks 'e's doing fine work, an' we'll let 'im think it,' was Tom Pink's mental injunction.

Coming on to the course proper *Captain* led by a full length from *Pieface*, who was travelling remarkably well. *Black Tulip* was half a neck behind *Pieface*, whilst *King's Lee*, *Nazi*, *Dingo Lad* and *Olary Boy* held even honours. The rest of the field pressed close.

At the Members' Stand *Captain* still led by a length - a big horse of stamina and grit. *Maid of the Moon* was slipping back, and Tom edged in nearer the rails.

There was the judge's box rushing towards them; now was gone by. Too late to spurt and try to edge on to the rails ahead of *Queen Kate*, before the first turn was reached, the turn to the long stretch beside the river. Clots of damp turf rose high from the leaders to fall among the ruck.

To the right the Maribyrnong River; on the left the frozen sea of human faces on the Flat. The fight for position began in earnest, *Pieface* was dropping back. *King's Lee* was battling with *Captain* for the lead. *Black Tulip* was edging in front of *Olary Boy*. A bright bay filly, her nostrils scarlet, was slipping up alongside *Olary Boy*. *Auburn Girl*, carrying a light weight, hugged the rails behind *Dingo Lad*.

A mile and a quarter to go! What the devil was young Hurley doing to let out *Pieface* like that? The fool! Did he want to bust the horse with a mile and a quarter yet to go? Look up, Hurley! What in hell - Keep - him - up!

Pieface had lurched outwards. He staggered. He - no, he

wasn't down. Gee - what a recovery! Hold him, Hurley, hold him! Gawd!

During two full seconds *Pieface* made the field appear as though it stood still. Then lightning seemed to strike him. All his strength vanished and he collapsed in a ball which rolled and slithered over the grass with terrific momentum! A short streak of brilliant red shot forward and outward from the brown mass.

Good! Hurley hadn't been nipped beneath his horse. Fallen horse and inert jockey were swept behind on the unrolling ribbon of the course.

'Heart failure!' a jockey screamed.

Heart failure, be jiggered! Cup runners didn't drop dead with heart failure. What ruddy rot!

Blast! He mustn't let that sort of thing distract this peculiarly floating mind, which was him, Tom Pink, from the one idea, the one purpose. Here was a race when the pace was on all the way, victory resting with the best stayer lying stretched out over two full miles.

Position was desirable, most desirable, especially before reaching the seven furlongs, but it was pace which would tell, for the horse guided by a rider having miles-deep knowledge of his mount, knowing to the last ounce what his mount had in him.

King's Lee was running nose to nose with *Captain*, but the wonderful New Zealand stallion revealed the effects of a rain-soaked course. *Black Tulip* was disputing place on the rails with *Nazi*, *Olary Boy* coming on a little on the outside of the black mare. The heads of *Auburn Girl*, *Wayside Belle* and *Dingo Lad* all were in the range of Tom's vision. The rhythmic drumming of eighty hoofs imperceptibly quickened.

At the seven *Nazi* moved out from the rails, and for the first time Tom relaxed the slight pressure on the reins. *Olary Boy* instantly spurted into the opening given, like a destroyer manoeuvring among battle cruisers. And then when *Olary Boy*'s head was level with *Nazi*'s rump, the latter's rider sharply swung his mount on to the rails again.

Catastrophe clutched at *Olary Boy*, and to prevent a bad jam preceding an ugly accident, Tom was compelled to pull his horse. For three to four seconds *Olary Boy* became like an anchored lightship.

Nine or ten horses slid on by *Olary Boy* during that unfortunate check. A horse immediately behind almost cannoned in a supreme effort to avoid collision, and when *Olary Boy* again ran into his stride it was seen that he had dropped back to 15th place.

'The dirty dog! Musta seen *Olary Boy*'s nose on his left. You wait, you water-drinking owl.'

Three-quarters of a mile to go, *King's Lee* leading the field with *Black Tulip* hanging to him like a limpet. The mighty *Captain* was tiring, being passed by the flying *Auburn Girl*. Just ahead *Dingo Lad*, *Black Princess* and *Sir Newton*, all running in a bunch. Well, here's so long you, *Red Rose*. See you after. And the same to you, whatever's your name. Hullo, *Sir Newton* - gettin' blow'd out? Well, what are you doing in a two-mile amble like this? Now - now! It's no good, *Dingo Lad*. Better give up now as later. That's right, Snozzler - just stop dreaming until we get in ahead of this funny thing they calls *Wayside Belle*.

Gleaming eyes in a mask - the brain which was Tom Pink, the brain which knew just what *Olary Boy* had left in him when four more furlongs remained to be covered.

Now against the rail, *Olary Boy* was among the first six, racing neck to neck with *Nazi*. To *Nazi*'s rider, as though it were the voice of Doom, Tom Pink screamed words:

'You balloon-faced devil's pimp! You jam me, you crayfish! I'm gonna chew yer nose off, bime by. Now, Snozzler, eat 'em alive oh!'

The leaders were sweeping into the straight, *Black Tulip* and *King's Lee* fighting it out on the rail, and at the end of the long, long turn, Tom steered *Olary Boy* off the rail to get a clear run.

Ahead rumbled thunder.

Captain was edging up on *Olary Boy*. His jockey was using his whip. The thunder burst out in volume like the thunder of water from a great dam. *Nazi* was going back - was gone. Auburn Girl was coming back. And so was *King's Lee*.

'Snozzler! Snozzler! You an' me's for it!'

They were into the sound storm. It was like stepping from a great stonebuilt house into the raging elements. The ethereal sound waves beat against their ears, sound clubs battering at them, battering them back.

'*Ba—tip! Ba—tip! Ba—tip! Ak—tip! Ak—tip! Black—tip! Black Tulip! Black Tulip! Black Tulip!*'

Vast cacophony resolving into two intelligible words.

And amidst this roaring tumult, to Tom the crackling of machine guns. The whips were going.

'Snozzler! Snozzler! No whip fer you, Snozzler!'

A furlong and a half . . .

'Snozzler—Snozzler—we're gonna do it—do it—do it!'

Slipping back—slipping back! *Auburn Girl* was slipping back, was level, was behind. Coming back—coming back! *King's Lee* was coming back, swaying his head. Green as grass—green as grass. The champ—green as grass—green as grass. Lookin' at the scenery—at the scenery. Ah—got you rotten—rotten—rotten. Come back, *Tulip—Tulip—Tulip.* Got you rotten—rotten—rotten.

One furlong . . .

Sound waves beat and clashed—beat and clashed—beat and clashed! O'ree—oi! A'ree—oi! *Olary* oi! *Olary Boy— Boy—Boy! Olary Boy—Boy—Boy! Olary Boy!*

On me own – on me own – on me own! They're all behind! They're all behind!

'*Olary Boy! Olary Boy!*' roared the crowd. 'Come on – Come on! Come on – come on!'

'We're gonna be there – we're gonna be there,' screamed a voice in Tom's ears, a voice he knew was his own. A heaving sea on either side rolled and tossed and roared:

'*Olary Boy - Olary Boy!*'

'I'm ridin' a winner—I'm ridin' a winner—I'm ridin' a winner! I knew it, knew it, knew it! Now —now—now, Snozzler—now—now—now——!'

Then suddenly lightning stuck—a dark green bolt! The earth split open—accepted Tom into its black cavern of mouth.

The thunderous words '*Olary-Boy*' became changed to an echo, vibrantly dying away into cosmic stillness. . .

'*Black Tulip! Black Tulip! Black Tulip! Bak—ip! Bak—ip! Ak—ip! Ak—Ip! Ip! Ip Ip.*'

19

Met Trouble

At the head of the dining table sat Old Masters; on his right, his son; to the left, Dick Cusack. Joyce hovered about them.

'The only satisfactory point in the whole disgraceful business is that Alverey's horse didn't win the Cup,' Old Masters was saying with his usual downrightness. 'I suppose your horses were poisoned? They didn't just drop dead?'

'I would be inclined to think that *Olary Boy* suddenly collapsed beneath the strain, almost at the winning post, if *Pieface* hadn't collapsed after having run only seven furlongs,' Roy replied steadily. 'I might have thought it about *Olary Boy*, despite the fact that horses having run in many races and being in constant training would most improbably not drop dead.'

'Hug-hum! Question is how were they poisoned; then, when was the poison administered? And then, what was the poison?'

'We'll know tomorrow how they were poisoned - and with what poison, and we might then be able to guess when they were poisoned,' Dick said, calm now that anti-climax had come.

'Was Hurley's life insured?'

'No personal insurance. His mother will receive

compensation under the Act, and I shall see that she is properly provided for,' Dick averred; then to burst out: 'My God - those swine want hanging if they're ever caught.'

'We'll leave that to Leader,' growled Old Masters; to add in grim after thought: 'Catching them, I mean, not hanging them.'

'Who's Leader?' demanded Dick.

Roy remembered putting the same question.

'He'll be here presently,' prevaricated Old Masters. 'Joyce, Mr. Cusack's glass.'

For a little while silence. Then:

'Your man seems to have got off lightly, Roy.'

'Yes, Dad. He was fortunate in escaping with no broken limbs. But the concussion he received might yet prove fatal. He was still comatose when I visited the private hospital just before coming in here.'

'By Heck, he rode well, Mr. Masters!' Dick put in. 'After getting in that jam with *Nazi* which put *Olary Boy* almost last, it was nothing less than marvellous the way he rode him into first place one furlong from home. He was easily a length ahead of *Black Tulip* when he went down.'

'Did the horse stagger much before he collapsed?'

'No. He simply dropped, and his speed sent him sliding along the turf for yards. How Pink escaped serious injury, I don't know.'

'Hug-hum! It is a terrible affair.'

'Diana is frightfully upset about it. The shock, just when *Olary Boy* was on the point of winning, was great. I'll ring up Tindale again after dinner.'

'Yes, Roy, do,' urged Old Masters. 'Confound it, Leader is late. Joyce, what time did he say he would be here?'

'Eight o'clock, sir. It is now—'

'I know the time. Hug-hum! Why cannot people be punctual? If I say I will be at a place at a certain time, at that place at that time I will be. Only, an accident would make me late.'

'An accident, Sir! Mr. Leader—'

'Who the devil asked you talk, Joyce,' the old man roared. 'Why mention Leader and an accident in the same breath? Don't answer me, Joyce. I won't have it.'

Dick regarded the butler curiously. He was a slight silver-haired man of sixty or thereabouts. His eyes were pale blue, but clear and steady. Now on his usually serene face agitation was very evident.

'I suppose you backed *Olary Boy*,' Old Masters said, with less vocal volume.

'I lost five hundred pounds on him,' Roy sighed.

'And I lost a thousand on him,' Dick added.

'What! Hug-hum! You wagered a thousand on him, Dick. I didn't know the price of wool was that much up and all taxes down.'

'And Diana, lost fifty on him, too,' Dick vouchsafed gloomily.

'You must have thought he was going to win.'

'He'd have won all right, Mr. Masters - if he hadn't been killed.'

'Still, a thousand is a lot of money. Hug-hum! Yes, Joyce, you may leave us. When Mr. Leader arrives show him in here.' And then when the door had softly closed behind the butler: 'I intend taking you two boys into my confidence. I will tell you a few interesting facts while we wait for Leader. Try those Havanas.'

The further the mystery of this man, Leader, deepened, the more Roy feel the strain. Memory of three faces revealed by an electric standard was vivid, but never had he dared ask his father how he came to be walking at night with his valet and that other man.

'Twelve years ago I was involved in an ugly blackmailing gang,' Old Masters proceeded. 'A very dear friend of mine had committed an indiscretion, a breath of which would have ruined him in his public life. He was not well off and far too poor to pay the blackmail; which was why he came to me.

'Not daring to take the matter to the police, I enlisted the services of Joyce, and, later on, the services of Leader, Joyce's brother-in-law. Leader then was a detective-sergeant, and he acted with us in a private capacity. Later, I took him out of the police force and engaged him as my own private detective.

'The head of the blackmailing gang was one Hellburg. We never saw him. The members of his gang were many and his four lieutenants were known by a peculiar arrangement of numbers - One of Four up to Four of Four.'

'It was one of them who signed the letter which Tom Pink found on the race pimp. He heard another addressed—'

'Yes, Roy. The same gang evidently are behind the attacks on *Olary Boy* and *Pieface*,' Old Masters went on, impatient of the interruptions. 'They are about the nastiest combination of black-guards you can imagine. We bested Hellburg on that occasion, but he hasn't forgotten or forgiven. Ah - has Leader arrived, Joyce?'

'No sir. There is a caller on the telephone.'

'Very well - switch him through.'

Old Masters leaned sideways in his chair and lifted the receiver from a desk instrument on its small table beside him.

Here in the dining-room, he could be switched through to the world by the house exchange in the hall.

'Ah - is that Mr. Masters?' inquired a soft voice, containing just the ghost of an accent.

'It is,' grunted the old man.

'This is Hellburg speaking from a public call-box,' went on the voice. 'I am sorry your Mr. Leader is late. I desire to say that he will be unable to call on you for some time. If you are anxious to see him you will find him right in the angle of Ryrie Place, off Queen Street. Make haste, I think he is very unwell and in need of attention. Oh - by the way, Mr. Masters, kindly refrain from poking your nose into my business in the future. Good-bye, I hope it will not be mere au revoir for your sake ...'

'D'you know Ryrie Place, off Queen Street?' Old Masters demanded with thin lips barely parted.

'Yes, I think I do, Dad.'

'Good! We'll go right away. We'll take your car, Roy. Leader has met trouble.'

'Who was that on the 'phone?'

'Hellburg.'

'What, the gang leader?'

'The same. Joyce,' to the butler who had answered the bell, 'my hat and coat, quick!'

'Is anything wrong, sir?' asked Joyce whilst helping his master into a heavy overcoat.

'Dunno. It's Leader in trouble.'

'Then may I accompany you, sir?' Joyce said, entreaty in his voice, alarm in his eyes.

Old Masters' optical glare softened, but his voice remained brittle.

'No. You will stay here. As you see, I have an excellent guard.'

'Very well, sir. Shall I get you your pistol?'

'No, not now. I think you had better clean and oil it, though. And if you still have your own, oil and clean that, too.'

'They are both ready for instant use, sir.'

'Hug-hum! The devil they are.'

'Yes, sir. If you will pardon me, sir, I have been anticipating trouble.'

'So have I, Joyce. Well - come along, you boys.'

Roy drove to Ryrie Place without experiencing difficulty. From the street its first right angle turn could be seen faintly, a distance of perhaps fifty yards. Midway between the Queen Street entrance and the right angle was one electric light, and, round the angle at some distance, another.

'Hellburg said Leader would be in the angle. Can you see him?' asked Old Masters.

'Not from here. Let's investigate,' Dick urged.

Side by side they marched into the dimly lit place, a canyon between tall business blocks. At the corner they stopped.

'You see him, do you?' asked the old man.

'What is that over there in the opposite angle?'

'Where? Yes, that looks like a standing man, lounging into the wall angle.'

They walked across the unevenly paved road. They then saw a man muffled in a dark overcoat and wearing a felt hat low over his eyes. There was something a little strange about this figure. His arms were not in the coat sleeves, although the coat was buttoned across his chest.

'Good evening,' Roy said shortly.

The man gave no reply.

Old Masters struck a match to assist the distant lights. They saw the man's sagged jaw. Dick lifted the felt hat, and they saw the wide, staring and glassy eyes.

'He's dead,' Roy whispered.

'And it's not Leader,' Old Masters gasped.

'Now, what's all this?' demanded a gruff, metallic voice from behind them.

20

Knifed!

The three men standing horror-stricken before the dead man propped naturally against the angle of meeting brick walls spun round when the gruffly put question fell on their ears.

'What's wrong here?' demanded the uniformed policeman.

'That man is dead, constable,' Old Masters said, steadily.

'Dead! How did he come by his death? D'you know?'

The questions were now barked. A flashlight was produced; its beam directed to the dreadful face plainly revealed now that the hat was all awry.

'And who are you? What are you doing here?'

'My name is Masters, officer,' The policeman was proffered a card, which he accepted and read. 'This is my son, Mr. Roy Masters, and this, Mr. Cusack.'

'Not the owners of *Olary Boy* and *Pieface*?'

'The same, officer.'

'And you, sir? Are you the proprietor of the Masters store?'

'The same. We were passing along Queen Street, and on impulse walked in here to view the rear of premises, the purchase of which we have been debating. Now, what are we going to do about the dreadful affair?'

'Ring the C. I. B., Russell Street, for the patrol.'

'Shall I do it?' asked Roy, astonished by his father's cool lying regarding the viewing of property for probable purchase.

'Yes, please,' assented the constable. Then, when he had gone: 'Must be foul play. People don't die naturally leaning against a wall and stay leaning against it. Wonder how he was killed. Don't touch him.'

The crowd in Queen Street passed the narrow entrance to the lane without suspecting the grim crime concealed by the small group waiting for the patrol car. Two men approached from the further end of the lane, examined the group with careless eyes, passed on into Queen Street.

Roy returned after an absence of two minutes.

'They're coming,' he said briefly.

'It seems to me the bird has been dead some time,' remarked the constable. 'Queerest thing ever I struck. Looks like his overcoat was put on him after he was dead, too.'

'Hug-hum! It's a beastly business altogether,' Old Masters said, regaining his former coolness. 'Confound it! I suppose now our time will be wasted with an inquest. I'm confoundedly sorry, Roy, I consented to your wish to see the property.'

Through the passing crowd they saw big, efficient men pushing their way. Reaching the entrance to the lane, one of them stopped to hold back the curious, who guessed what they were. The remaining three hurried to the group awaiting them.

'What's wrong, constable?'

'Man dead,' was the reply.

A powerful torch aided the light from the distant electrics.

'Dead all right. But what's keeping him up? Any of you touched him?'

'I lifted his hat to look at him,' Dick said.

'When?'

'When we found him.'

'When was that?'

'Several minutes ago. I should say about half a minute before the constable came along.

'And that will be five minutes and about 15 seconds,' added the constable, looking up from his watch.

'Well, that makes it nine-ten p.m...'

One gently pulled the man forward - and the dead man fell forward stiffly into the detective's arms. He laid him down.

'Why, he's as stiff as a crutch,' he gasped. 'He wasn't killed five minutes ago.'

'No - and he didn't prop himself against the wall to die comfortably from heart failure. Open up his overcoat.'

'Hullo - he's got two overcoats on. Ah - look! He was knifed over the heart. And to hide the blood on his grey overcoat the black coat was put on him.'

'Yes, but only recently. After rigor mortis had set in. He was killed away from here hours ago. Must have been brought here and propped up against that wall.'

'Looks like it,' said he who appeared to be the senior. 'Did you bring him here?'

'Of course not. What next?' Old Masters burst out sarcastically. 'D'you think I've got so much time on my hands I can waste some of it carting corpses about?'

'Mr. Masters of the stores, Mr. Roy Masters and Mr. Cusack - they say they are,' put in the constable. 'Say they were down here looking at the back of some property they were thinking of buying. This is the card Mr. Masters senior produced.'

The beam of the powerful torch was directed full into Old Master's face.

'So it is,' a voice said behind the torch. The voice became more conciliatory. 'This is a bad business, sir.'

'I don't need to be told that,' Old Masters snapped. 'The best thing to do now is to get in touch with the Chief Commissioner. If possible, I don't wish to be dragged into it.'

'I'm afraid that can't be helped, Mr. Masters. A bit of bad luck. Is that your car at the kerb - a green single seater?'

'No. It belongs to my son.'

'Well, that seems to prove you didn't sneak into the lane from the other end, bringing the dead man with you.'

'As a matter of fact,' Roy put in. 'I remember the owner of the tobacco shop on the right of the entry standing in his doorway. He might remember seeing us come here - without the burden of a dead man.'

'All right - we'll question him, as a matter of form. Hicks, ring headquarters for a photographer. Searle, you accompany these gentlemen to Russell Street and get their statements. Identification is unnecessary, because I recognise Mr. Masters.'

Old Masters snapped and roared all the way to Russell Street, Dick and Roy offering but rare comment, and both marvelling at the old man's determination to withhold the telephone conversation with a man named Hellburg - wondering at the reason why the information was withheld and utterly mystified by the whole affair. After being led to expect to find, or meet with a man named Leader, they had been confronted by the dead body of a man, who was quite a stranger to Old Masters.

It happened that the Chief Commissioner and Old Masters were well known each to the other, both being members of the same club, although the latter had seldom visited it during the last few years. At the old man's urgent call, the Chief Commissioner hurried to headquarters. Having received the patrol leader's report, he said, gravely:

'It is all most unfortunate for you.'

'Of course it is! Hug-hum! Are we going to be dragged into this affair, Loxton?'

'I can't very well see how you can be kept out of it,' the Commissioner replied reluctantly. 'Still, perhaps you may be excused from a most unpleasant duty; but you, Mr. Roy and you, Mr. Cusack, will have to attend as having discovered the body.' Then, with a smile, he added to Old Masters: 'Don't worry, Masters, we'll leave the burden to younger and stronger shoulders.'

Again on the road, headed for St. Kilda, Roy said impatiently:

'Why did you keep back the real reason we went to that lane, Dad? That man Hellburg, or his associates, must have done it.'

'They did it all right, Roy.'

'But why did you keep back that information?' pressed the younger man.

'Because I don't want to be asked about Hellburg. Because I don't want to be asked how I came to know him. That other matter is dead and buried. I hope to goodness Leader has turned up in our absence.'

'What do you think was the reason Hellburg told you

where to meet Leader and then confronted us with a man not Leader; do you know?'

'I don't. It beats me.'

Conversation lapsed until they drew up before Old Masters' house.

'You boys come in and have a drink. We'll talk things over.'

Joyce opened the hall door to admit them.

'Mr. Leader is in the library, sir,' Joyce said with gratification in his voice. 'He arrived only a few minutes after you left.'

'Good. I think he's lucky to be alive,' growled the old man, leading the way along the deeply carpeted corridor. And as Joyce was busy hanging up overcoats and hats, it was Old Masters who opened the library door.

'Well, Leader, what kept you?' he demanded, as he entered the room. 'Why——'

He broke off suddenly, with a gasp as the others pushed by him, gazing at the figure before him. It was Roy who first realised the truth.

'Good God – He's dead!'

21

Too Old

When Roy spoke again his voice was quite low.

'Close and lock the door, Dick,' he commanded, with more than a hint of his father's brusqueness.

A big, robust man with iron-grey hair and moustache was sprawled in a great lounge chair facing the door. He was dressed in a neat serge suit. For his size, his feet were small and were shod with high-grade shoes.

'Is this your Mr. Leader?' Roy asked, as they stood and stared at the motionless figure.

Old Masters nodded. The twin horrors of this night appeared at last to have struck him dumb. Virility had departed from him, and his age became far more accentuated.

'Look! The window is wide open,' Dick pointed out. 'And, see - someone has been rummaging in all the drawers.'

'Touch nothing - nothing, Dick. Keep any valuables here, Dad? What about the safe?'

Old Masters crossed to a wall tapestry, swept it aside to reveal the door of a compact steel safe wide open, the several drawers pulled out, their contents scattered about the floor of the alcove in which the safe rested.

'Robbery!' he said slowly - to add, as though it were an afterthought: 'And murder. Two murders. I must think - I must think.'

'We must allow others to do the thinking, Dad,' Roy rapped out. 'We must report this to the police at once.'

The reply came slowly.

'No - no! That we mustn't do, Roy. They would want to know too much.'

Roy swung round, wide-eyed, in amazement.

'What? Here we have a burglar ransacking the room. Enter your man, Leader. He is killed by the burglar and the burglar escapes. Why, in the name of commonsense, mustn't we call the police?' he cried.

'I don't know - I don't know, Roy,' mumbled the older man. 'It might be all as simple as you state - it might not. Look here! You two young fellows go home. Leave this awful affair to Joyce and to me. We'll bide our time - and later we'll carry poor Leader some distance from the house and set him down for the police to find.'

'But that'll only make matters worse,' Roy gasped, astounded by his father's fantastic plan. 'The thing's been done here in your house, and it will have to be reported, Dad. The police have got to know about the telephone conversation you had with the man whose name you say is Hellburg. They've got to know just why we went to Ryrie Place. And they've got to be called here at once.'

Old Masters was a pathetic caricature of the once stern, efficient and clear-headed business magnate. Two hours ago he had looked barely sixty years of age. Now he appeared to be verging on eighty. His hands trembled. His lips quivered. And into his eyes crept dull shadows of mental fatigue.

'All right, Roy. I'll leave it all to you,' he stammered, in quavering tones. 'It has been too much - too much. You telephone Roy - we'll go to the dining-room for a drink and a smoke.'

'Good! I feel gone in the knees, Mr. Masters,' Dick said seriously. 'Another shock like this, and I'll go in the nut, too.'

'Touch nothing here,' Roy requested, as he unlocked and opened the door for the others to pass out.

The butler was lurking in the passage.

'Whisky, Joyce. In the dining-room,' the old man ordered.

'Yes, sir. And Mr. Leader?'

'Do what you are told, Joyce, damn you,' cursed the old man, who was showing signs of recovery again. He strode in ahead of Dick, his shoulders bowed, his body hunched forward.

'I am too old for all this sort of thing Dick,' he muttered, as they entered the dining-room. 'Make it a stiff one, Joyce.'

'Yes, sir, certainly.'

'And after Mr. Cusack, have a drink yourself. You'll be wanting it.'

'Thank you, sir, very much,' the astonished butler concurred, with lifted eyebrows. 'Mr. Leader—'

'What time did Leader arrive?'

'Well - you left, sir, at eight-thirty. It would be about twenty minutes to nine o'clock.'

'When you showed him into the library did you enter the room yourself?'

'No, sir. I didn't show him to the library. He said I needn't bother, because he had asked me and I had informed him I was taking supper, sir. I suggested refreshment, sir, and he declined. He said he would be busy tabulating his notes. But why, sir? Is there anything wrong?'

Old Masters' face was grim.

'He's dead, Joyce,' was his brief answer.

'Dead! Mr. Leader dead, sir?'

The butler's tone was that of a man dazed or incredulous.

'Yes, Joyce,' the old man said quietly, as he took a sip from his glass. 'Yes, Leader is dead ... A cigar, you fool; and a match.'

The butler's hands visibly trembled when they held out the cigar box. They trembled a little more when he struck a match on the box. And then, his cigar alight, Old Masters patted the man's black-coated arm, saying kindly:

'Steady, Joyce - steady. Since we have been away the library has been burgled - and poor Leader has been murdered.'

The butler's lips drew outward.

'Hellburg,' he said.

'It may not be - but I think it is, Joyce. But you'll keep your opinion to yourself.'

'Certainly, sir. Oh, Mr. Masters! My poor sister.'

'You must go to her directly the confounded police have finished with us,' Then to Roy, who had entered the room: 'Well?'

'They are coming, Dad. I rang up the Commissioner at his private house. He is coming too.'

'Thank you, Roy. It was a good idea. I'll be able to talk to him better than his policemen.'

'I'm deuced sorry you've been dragged into this, old boy,' Roy told Dick, who had been a curious spectator of the little act between master and man.

'Don't talk nonsense, Roy. I'm beginning to think I shall take an interest in this night's work. Anyway, I've long promised myself a holiday.'

'A fine holiday it well be,' grunted Old Masters. 'Joyce, go along to the hall and be ready to open to the police. If the cook and maids haven't gone to bed, pack 'em off at once.'

'They all have retired, sir.'

'Feeling better, Dad?' Roy asked.

'Yes. I was knocked to pieces for a moment. Now listen, you boys. Don't you mention to anyone about Hellburg ringing me up. You'll allow me to say all that's necessary to the police. You understand that?'

'But to keep back ...'

'I shall not keep back anything but Hellburg's telephone message,' said Old Masters, 'or rather, I shall keep back Hellburg's name. I must give the message itself. Ah - here they are,' he added, as footsteps sounded outside.

A moment later three plainclothes men were shown in by Joyce. The leader stepped forward.

'Trouble here, sir? I am Sergeant Love.'

'I am glad you've arrived. Roy, offer these gentlemen refreshment.'

Of the three, only the sergeant accepted.

'We were out this evening, sergeant, and during our absence ex-Detective-Sergeant Leader, who is in my employ, called on business. Knowing the run of the house, he did not trouble my butler to show him to the library. We returned at twenty minutes after ten, and on learning that Leader was in the library, we went to that room,' Old Masters paused, and then continued. 'We then discovered Leader in one of the easy chairs - dead.'

The curt announcement visibly staggered the visitors. Trouble of some sort they had anticipated. Folk do not summon police for fun. But - this sounded like real trouble -

and their leader's expression was grim as he said, gravely, 'Dead, you say? Then we'd better have a look at him.'

'Take them along, Roy, I will stay here.'

Quite still, the old man and Dick listened to their retreating footsteps. They heard a door open, and quietly close. Dick crossed to the dining room door and closed that. When he returned he drew a chair beside Old Masters. Speaking, he was very serious.

'This is pretty ghastly, Mr. Masters,' he said. 'Of course, Roy was right in yelling for the police. Yet, if it hadn't been for his wise head I would have seconded your vote in taking Leader away and leaving the poor chap somewhere.'

'We might have regretted it, Dick,' Old Masters objected. 'It was a panic suggestion, after all.'

'Well, anyway, I want you to know that you can count on me at all times. This Leader - was he engaged on investigation work for you?'

'He was. He was looking into the business of the doping of *Olary Boy*. And – mark me – the people behind that, and behind the killing of your horse and of *Olary Boy*, are Hellburg and his crowd.'

'Oh! Then I'm mighty glad I decided to pull my weight. I am pretty sore about young Hurley and *Pieface* and I am sore, too, about *Olary Boy*. My thousand pounds were a lost bet and I never squeal; but *Olary Boy* would have won the Cup, and Roy would have been entitled to claim Diana.

'But you are in love with Diana, too, aren't you?'

'Yes.'

Dick looked down on the rug at his feet. After a little silence, he said: 'Yes - I love Diana with all that's in me. But we agreed, Roy and I. *Pieface* never had an earthly. *Olary Boy*

135

was a certain winner when he collapsed. Had he lived half of one more minute, Roy could have claimed Diana. And, because I think Diana loves him now, she would gladly have accepted him. I never squeal at a fair and square gamble, but' (and Old Masters noted the blazing blue eyes) 'I am squealing now over *Olary Boy* not winning, because of dirty methods. Which is—'

'There is a ring on the telephone, sir. Shall I put it through?' asked Joyce suddenly from the doorway.

Old Masters nodded, Joyce disappeared. Old Masters lifted the receiver against his ear, and the next instant Dick saw his body tense.

'Mr. Masters?' queried a soft voice.

'Well!'

'Oh - I rang you up to say how sorry I am to have got you involved needlessly with the affair at Ryrie Place,' went on the soft, languid voice. 'You see, the man I took on in place of Two of Four, now serving a long sentence is rather new. It appears that last night Mr. Leader was a little uneasy in his mind, and he induced a perfectly innocent person to exchange his new grey overcoat and nice hat for an old and shabby overcoat and a battered hat. The exchange was not noticed by the new Two of Four.

'Therefore, when, as planned, you were out of the house tonight Three of Four was much surprised when Mr. Leader entered your library whilst Three of Four was examining your papers. Realising the mistake committed by Two of Four, he at once rectified it.

'Are you still there, Mr. Masters? Yes? Well, a few words of advice. Don't meddle with my affairs, or your peace will be disturbed. And don't employ anyone else, because removals

I do not favour, as a rule. I trust you understand me?'

'The hangman will settle your affairs, Hellburg,' Old Masters roared fiercely. 'You—'

'Life, of course, is very uncertain, Mr. Masters,' the hateful voice went on calmly. 'I refer to your existence as well as to my own. Goodbye - or shall it be, au revoir?'

22

Very Strange

A week passed, a week filled with anxiety for Old Masters, for his son, and for Dick Cusack; and in lesser degree for Diana Ross. On the evening of the day that the inquiry was held on the killing of the two racehorses, Dick and Roy, with Tom Pink, arrived to dine with Mr. Tindale and his ward.

'Are you quite recovered?' Diana asked the jockey.

'Yes, Miss Ross. I came a terrible cropper off'n ole Snozzler, but I'm all right now, thank you,' was the reply.

'It was a mercy you weren't killed.'

'It were that, Miss,' Tom agreed, his hairless head shining like a billiard ball, his recently shaven face glowing like a pale tomato. 'But I wouldn't have minded the buster if *Olary Boy* 'adn't been killed.'

'It was dreadful – but-but – do you know what's happened?'

Tom Pink grinned bashfully.

'Yes, Miss. I've lost me stuttering, but I'd 'ave sooner kept me stutter than lose ole Snozzler. Me and somebody is gonna 'ave a word or two in private some day.'

'Well, I hope you will allow me to be present, Mr. Pink,' Diana said, her eyes glinting.

Tom looked his doubting mind.

'Perhaps, Miss, if you was there I wouldn't enjoy myself so much,' he stated seriously.

'Then I shall keep away. Tell me, someone, all about the inquiry at the Racing Club's headquarters.'

'Box on, Roy. You're a better talker,' urged Dick.

'It was all pretty rotten,' Roy said in preamble. 'The day after the Melbourne Cup the chief vet conducted an autopsy on *Olary Boy* and *Pieface*. Hullo! Here is Mr. Tindale. You are just in time to hear an account of the inquiry, Mr. Tindale.'

'Good! I am most anxious to hear all about it,' averred the squatter. 'How d'you, Dick. How d'you, Tom. Glad to see you about again. Feeling fit?'

'All right, thanks, Mr. Tindale.'

'Good - again! Now, Roy, fire ahead.'

'I was just saying that the chief veterinary surgeon examined *Olary Boy*, and *Pieface* the morning after the race,' Roy explained. 'He found that both horses had been poisoned by an agent in the neurotoxic division. What it was precisely he was unable to state. He called in the Government toxicologist, who, after making blood tests, gave it as his opinion that the horses appeared to have died from snake venom. The venom of the majority of our Australian snakes would account for the action of the poison introduced.

'Exactly what the poison was, he couldn't say. It had attacked the nerve centres, causing failure of the heart. It would have had little if any effect on the respiratory organs - which accounts for the sudden death unaccompanied by any warning symptoms.'

'Very strange,' remarked the squatter. 'How was the poison administered?'

'That, too, was not ascertained,' Roy replied. 'They made

a thorough examination of the horses' hides, and discovered no mark, no sign of a hypodermic being used.'

'Then it must have been administered in their food.'

'That was the opinion given by both the vet, and the specialist.'

'It wasn't given 'em in their tucker, as I said,' Tom declared, heatedly. 'They oughta 'ave skinned them 'orses to make proper search for needle marks.'

'Perhaps you are right, Tom. Anyway, they did not, and it's too late now. Nat Sparks described all the precautions he took to safeguard the horses from interference, and the president afterwards said he could have done nothing more. Tom, here, stated that he never left *Olary Boy* from the moment he was taken from the stables.'

'Hum! It is a horrible business,' Mr. Tindale said slowly. 'And as the horses were deliberately poisoned, young Hurley met his end through foul play?'

'Decidedly. Whoever got at *Pieface* is guilty of his death.'

'Well, I sincerely hope they find the criminal, Roy. How is your father standing all this turmoil?'

'He's better. But the double shocks we three received the same night tried him much. It has all made him feel his years.

That dinner was wholly successful for Tom Pink amused and entertained them with quaint anecdotes of his racing life and of horses. Before they left for the show he furtively and mysteriously gave Diana a sealed envelope, and when, hours later in the privacy of her room, she opened it, she found a scrawled message which ran:—

'Meet me Cathedral corner eleven tomorrow.
It is most important. Please tell no one.'

23

The Police

It was not without considerable thought that Diana decided to acquiesce in Tom Pink's urgent request to meet him at the Cathedral corner opposite the Flinders Street station entrance, for in all the circumstances the assignation was something in the nature of an adventure.

She was about to cross to the Cathedral corner, when Tom Pink touched her arm restrainingly.

'Thank you for comin', Miss,' he said with particular earnestness. 'I've got to talk to you an' 'ere's no place. Will you come to a cafe with me? Cupper tea or somethink?'

'Why, yes Tom. That is a good idea. You may take me to a nice place at the top-end of Collins Street.'

'Too far, Miss. Too many people might see us walkin' there,' he countered quickly - and she noticed how sharply he examined each of the many people passing by. 'There's a little place close 'andy that would do us. You game?'

'Why, yes, if you'd rather,' she agreed, made curious by his obvious excitement which, in a measure, was communicated to her. She was escorted to one of the cheaper tea places and was pleasurably surprised to find that Pink's manners were not slurred as was his speech. He sought her permission to select a corner table and moved a chair for her. With tea and cakes between them, he said:

'I want you to lend me fifty quid. Will you?'

'Well - that's a lot of money, Mr. Pink,' Diana murmured, remembering Roy's account of Tom's flirtations with John Barleycorn.

He shrewdly guessed her thoughts, and produced a small roll of Treasury notes.

'I know, Miss,' she was told simply. 'For weeks an' munse I've been saving for a god ole beano with Jack Barnett directly after the Melbourne Cup, but things 'as 'appened to scratch that. Look - 'ere's eighteen quid of the seventy I got off'n Mr. Roy, an fifty of it I didn't spend on meself.

'Now, listen. You remember the time *Olary Boy* got doped when I thought it was you and that foreign gent? Well, of course, I noo' the people be'ind that was connected with the bloke calling 'isself Three of Four; who wrote to the bloke wot was to give me five quid for certain information which 'e didn't. And I reckoned if I could get 'old of a partic'lar bloke I once noo', 'e might be able to give me a lead.

'Yesterdee morning I 'ooked up to 'im. You see, Miss, it's like this. My ole man was a sooner. He'd sooner do anythink crook than honest. An' so would his pals. This bloke I wanted was one of them. I says to 'im— "I'm kinda interested in a bloke callin' 'isself Three of Four and another bloke whose moniker is Two of Four." 'E says—"Forget it. It ain't a healthy interest." I says: "My 'ealth's gonna be orl right, don't worry. There's two blokes I'm wantin' won't feel 'ealthy when I gets me gnashers into 'em."

''E 'ums and 'ahs for a bit, Miss. Then 'e says: "You workin' for the D's?" When I tells 'im I didn't arst for no insults, he says: "Look 'ere, Tom. I remember seein' you when you was so 'igh. I knew yor ole man, one of the straightest boys who ever lived. I don't want to hear of you bein' corpsed, as I will quick if you mucks about with the crowd you're interested in, see? I'm tellin' you nothin".'

'So I pulls out one wad and peels off nineteen quid and says: "'Ere's fifty of the best for what you can tell me." That fetched 'im and 'e spilled the beans, which was considerable.

'But, you understand Miss, givin' 'im that fifty makes me a bit short for what I want to do. No - wait a minute. I'm gonna get them blokes wot killed pore ole Snozzler. I know 'ow to get 'em. And I knows wot I'm up against - gents 'oo wouldn't qualify to be no nurse-maids.'

'Leave it all alone, Tom. Let it drop. Let the police manage Tom,' Diana said earnestly.

'The police! Why my ole man easy beat the police, and 'e 'ad no more brains than me or you. The police! They're orl right for pinchin' drunks or orderin' 'em out of town. No, this is a little job for me to do. Mr. Roy and Mr. Cusack is as sore as I am, but I'm not saying anythink to either of 'em, and you mustn't either. It's to keep Mr. Roy out of it that I've come to you for fifty quid. I know all about 'im an' you, Miss, an' good luck to 'im. 'E's a white man, 'e is, an' I'm draggin' 'im into no nasty corner where 'e might get a knife or a bullet, see.'

'And where you might get the same, Tom.'

'Unlikely, 'cos I can use meself a bit and I know me onions when it comes to crooks.'

'Leave it all alone, Tom,' Diana pleaded.

The jockey shook his hairless head.

'No, Miss. I'm gonna go for them swine wot did *Olary Boy* in,' she saw his bottom lip tremble, watched the tears gather into his eyes. 'You see, Miss, it's like this. I'm terrible fond of 'orses. P'haps it's becos' I ain't nothing to look at, and the tarts won't look at me. A man's got to be fond of somethink, ain't 'e? Well, I gets fond of 'orses. And I never got no fonder of a 'orse than I did of *Olary Boy.* He was that cute, 'e was. And when they did 'im in, it made me terrible sore. You lend me the fifty and tell no one nothink. I'll pay it back, straight!'

'I am not at all worried about that, Mr. Pink,' Diana hastened to assure him. 'But to me it seems so foolish of you to risk your life among those terrible men who hesitate at nothing. As I have already said - leave it all to the police.'

'It can't be done that way, Miss,' Tom said, grimly determined. 'With or without that loan I'm boxin' on.'

'Very well,' Diana sighed. 'If you will come with me to the bank, I'll draw the money for you.'

'You will? Thanks very much, Miss. But I'd rather stay here whiles you go to the bank, gets the money an' comes back. You see, them crooks know me by sight, some of 'em by feel, an' it won't go for them to see you with me.'

'All right,' Diana assented, rising. 'I'll not be long.'

A quarter of an hour later she was with Tom again, and gave him the money in pound notes.

'Now, remember, Miss: I'm gonna go into smoke,' he said. 'If Mr. Roy wants to know where I am, you lead 'im to think I got bush sick and cleared off back to Noo South. An' do orl you can to stop 'im and Mr. Cusack from botherin' about them Three of Fours. They're been goin' for years, that push, an' they're the toughest mob ever known by the underworld. No one knows 'oo the leader is. No one crosses 'em. So long, Miss, and many thanks. I'll pay this money back——'

'Oh - don't think of that now, Mr. Pink. If you should

want any more I'll willingly let you have it.'

'Thanks again, Miss. An' don't forget - say nothing to no one about me. Understand - no one!'

'Not a soul, Tom.'

'Good! Well, hooroo, Miss, and thank you again. I'll stop 'ere and give you five minutes' start.'

She held out a daintily gloved hand which he took into his huge paw:

'Good-bye, Tom, and good luck.'

'Good-bye, Miss. If you appears to see any blokes walking the streets with their ears chewed orf, it's me wot's done it. And, mum's the word.'

Her emotions very much mixed, Diana reached the street and crossed to the safety zone to catch her tram. In the tram she remembered having called the jockey Tom, when first she had rigidly clung to the Mr. Pink. It was ten minutes to one when she reached home.

24

Mother Hubbard

The senior officer engaged in investigating the twin murders was face to face with an unscalable wall. No one could be found who had seen a man or men enter Ryrie Place, carrying a burden likely to be a human body. Hundreds of interviews took place between detectives and people whose daily business took them to Ryrie Place, without resulting in a single fact, or even a theory, as to how the dead man had been propped in the wall angle. Mortell had died as he had lived, inconspicuously; dying mysteriously after having lived mysteriously on the fringe of Melbourne's underworld.

As for the tragedy in Old Masters' library, it, too, provided an amazing scarcity of clues. Not one fingerprint of Leader's murderer was found on furniture, window glass or safe. No article had been dropped by the burglar. There had been but slight, if any, struggle - and if a struggle, no evidence remained, no sound of it had reached the butler's ears.

'It is my opinion,' Sub-Inspector Dawson told the chief of his branch, 'that those two allied crimes have been carried out by the push who killed the fellow who ran the inside of the dope traffic, and who issued the fake ten-pound notes three years ago. We've never got a line on 'em yet, and whoever is at the head of the gang is deuced clever and not known to us.'

'They'll give us a lead sooner or later, Dawson,' was the chief's opinion. 'They always overstep the constable at some time. Haven't come across those two birds who, with the bird just out of jug, were taking that jockey for a ride?'

'Nary a birdseye view.'

'They're in it. I'll lay a quid to ten bob.'

'I agree. I think, too, that Old Masters hasn't come quite clean about those 'phone calls.'

'Oh - what makes you think that?'

'I can't tell you. If I was a woman I'd say it was intuition. Blast! When there's not a single line leading to anywhere it makes life damned uninteresting?'

Life might have been a little more interesting to Sub-Inspector Dawson had he known all the facts relating to Hellburg's two telephone calls. What he did not know also equalled in importance what he did know.

He did not know that Old Masters' telephone caller was known as Hellburg and that the strange cognomens of his four lieutenants ranged from One of Four to Four of Four. Not that he would have received much assistance had he known all this; but it would have been comforting, and most certainly the search for the men who tried to take Tom Pink for a ride would have been intensified.

And now Tom Pink was touching the fringe of the genuine underworld having been admitted on probation to Mother Hubbard's Cupboard.

The friend to whom he had paid fifty pounds for certain information piloted a disreputable piece of human flotsam, which was Tom Pink, along an alley running parallel with a certain street in an inner suburb, and after giving an elaborate system of passwords, finally conducted Tom into a large basement room, where men and women were sitting at tables, eating, drinking liquor, or playing cards.

The air was thick with tobacco smoke. A few careless glances were passed at Tom by the over-suspicious; the rest of the motley company were confident that no stranger could possibly pass through the efficient guards. For here was a veritable thieves' kitchen, a club where all kinds of crime were planned, where the dope wholesalers distributed snow to their runners, and where foregathered men 'in smoke' who, not desiring to walk abroad by day, repaired to this place to spend a convivial hour among friends.

The presiding goddess was Mother Hubbard, who spent most of her time in a little box-like office built into one corner. As the priest is the repository of the sins of his flock, so was this woman the confidant and the banker of the underworld.

'Now don't yous forget I'm finished,' Pink was reminded by his conductor of the evening. 'I've earnt me extra ten quid.'

'Don't worry, Larry,' Tom said, leaving his companion at one of the tables to make his way to the 'office'.

It was not a large 'office'. On a table were several little bowls containing silver and copper coins of the realm, and a small tin box containing Treasury notes. Before the table was seated a woman whose features were so debauched with cosmetics as to render any estimate of her age impossible.

'Good night, Mum. A word or two with you,' Tom said, leering down at the painted face in which two beady eyes examined him.

'Well, you're having them, ain't you?' she countered with a faint Irish brogue.

'I bin away from Melbourne nigh five years, and then I never 'ad time to see you. I'm Tom Brown.'

'Not old Tom Brown's son? Not the little feller belonging to Tom Brown who was hanged at Pentridge?'

'The same,' Tom Pink affirmed.

25

Dented Three Heads

Mother Hubbard and jockey stared each at the other, the woman noting Tom's soiled clothes and grubby, unshaven face. As though in rebellion at having to grow, the bristles appeared to sprout in clumps like tees on a golf course.

'Well—well—well!' at last explained the woman proprietor of this secret den. A man came in to settle his check and was asked to send 'Ted'. In turn 'Ted' was despatched for 'Jimmy', and 'Jimmy' proved to be a youth obviously far advanced in tuberculosis. He was ordered to 'take over', and Tom was invited to enter a room off the office. In this dowdy apartment he was invited to be seated opposite, and so close to the woman that their knees almost touched.

'I just cum along to see you, that's all,' Tom informed Mother Hubbard; then to add as though it were an after thought: 'And to git some information.'

'You have come to a funny place to get information. This is not a news exchange.'

'No? Anyway, I'm 'ere.'

'Who brought you?'

'Larry the Fly. I paid 'im a tenner.'

'You did? You must be flush! What do you want to know?'

'I want ter know 'oo the blokes are calling themselves,

Two of Four and Three of Four, an' oo's be'ind 'em. That's all.'

'Not much, Tom, is it?'

'No - easy spilled.'

'You workin' for the police?'

'As far as the police goes, I'm follering in father's footsteps.'

'All the same, I'm telling you nothing other than to advise you to watch yourself.'

Tom Brown, alias Tom Pink, regarded Mother Hubbard with a peculiarly cynical smile, and the woman, whose gaze never left his face, momentarily caught her breath in a barely audible gasp.

'Don't smile at me like that, Tom. It-it reminds me of someone,' she pleaded in tones which made of her painted face a hideous caricature. For a moment, the cold calculating hardness vanished. But only for an instant. Abruptly she rose to her feet, to say: 'I'm getting old, but life is sweet even to Mother Hubbard.'

'Sit down again,' Tom commanded, his eyes little points of livid grey. 'You 'aven't listened yet to what I want.' And then when the woman sat down: 'I know orl about you, Mother 'Ubbard; all 'bout regardin' a certain time. My ole man was 'anged in Pentridge for snuffling a bloke wot planted snow in your room 'cos he was jealous of my ole man. If it 'adn't bin for a silly lover's tiff 'im and you would 'ave bin spliced. Now wouldn't you?'

Mother Hubbard nodded her peroxided head.

'I'll go back a bit just to show you wot I know, ' Tom went on. 'My old man married my ole woman over that tiff between 'im an' you. Why, I don't know; you might. The first time I remember you, you was livin' not far from 'ere. I uster to be sent to you on the q.t. with letters from my ole man, and you uster gimme lollies at first and then sixpences after I growed a bit.

'I woke up to wot was goin' on between you an' 'im. You was still in love with 'im and 'e with you, an' the only decent thing 'e ever did in 'is life was to stick more or less, to my ole woman an' me. You an' 'im was at the pictures when I seen Mossy Light cum out of your room, 'im using a skeleton key. I knew Mossy 'ad no time for you 'cos you wouldn't leave me ole man for 'im.

'You know orl this but I'm just tellin' you for a bit of fun. When I sees Mossy lock your door with a skeleton, wot did I do? I went round an' tells Lena about Mossy, an' Lena used her key to get us into your room. Under your mattress we finds two bottles of snow and three tins of opium, and we 'adn't bin gorn out five minutes when the D's arrives. Mossy 'aving planted the stuff on you, he sools on the D's. An' if it 'adn't bin for me, you'd have got a possible five years.

'Course, I wouldn't have split to the ole man if I 'ad thought he was gonna lose 'is block and go for Mossy like a bull at a petticoat on a line. Still 'e did, an' 'e corpsed Mossy 'cos of you. You loved me ole man then, didn't you? An' memory ain't stone cold even now, is it? I never took after me ole man in looks, but some uster say I did look like 'im when I smiled.

'It seems ter me that takin' it by and large you owe me somethink—Chick.'

Mother Hubbard started back as though he had struck her. Her eyelids half closed down, then to flash upwards to reveal the blazing blue orbs.

'Don't you call me that name,' she said, her voice suddenly shrill.

'Well - me ole man uster call you that when 'e kissed you, didn't 'e?'

'Let be,' she gasped. 'God! To think I'd have all that brought out of the past when I was at last putting it away! I own that I owe you a lot. What is it you want to know?'

'I want ter know w'o the bloke is behind the men calling theirselves Two of Four and Three of Four.'

'I don't know.'

'You're a liar!'

'All right. But I don't know. What do you want to know for?'

'Me an' them 'as a slight argument to settle over doping a cuppler 'orses.'

'What have you to do with doped horses?'

During a little time-space, Tom scrutinised the highly rouged and powdered face and the brilliant scarlet lips of this scarlet woman. And then he slowly said:—

'My ole man committed murder 'cos he loved you. I'm gonna go nearly as far 'cos I loved a poor ole 'orse wot was doped. Yer see, I was on top of *Olary Boy* when 'e 'ad the Melbourne Cup in the bag.'

'O-oh! You're a jockey? You go by the name of Tom—'

'Just so. No need to shout the name.'

'And I suppose you are sore because you sunk a wad on him?'

'I put twenty notes on him, but that's nothink. I loved ole Snozzler, and I'm gonna get evens with the blokes wot done 'im in. Where do I hook up with 'em?'

'I can't tell you.'

'Liar again. You know. You know every crook in Melbourne, an' every crook's lay. Come on - spill the beans. You owe me that much.'

'You leave them alone, Tommy,' urged the woman, unconsciously using the derivative she always had used to the boy. 'That crowd are the toughest of 'em all. They've already got you in the gun, and if you take my advice you'll leave Melbourne as soon as you know how.'

'Nothin' doin',' Tom said steadily. 'I chewed one bloke's ears an' I dented three 'eads with a mulga waddy, but that ain't enough - not for me, any 'ow.'

'All the same. I'll telling you nothing, Tommy. When you're up against them you're up against something hard. Now you get out, and keep out while your health's good. That is how I'm going to repay you. Givin' you what you want - that wouldn't be payin you.'

They rose together.

'All right. Then I get to where I'm goin' round another corner, but I'll get there all right.'

'You may go there how you like, but you won't go there through me. I must get back to my office. You'll go out to Larry the Fly, and tell him to get you clear of this place quick an' lively.'

'I'll go when I'm ready to go.'

Mother Hubbard drew close to her visitor.

'You — fool!' she said bitingly. 'Can't you understand that if those mugs outside knew who you were, they'd guess your business, and there's others would know in five minutes. And then you'd never get to see daylight again.'

'That's all right I bested 'em once, and I can again. I'm gonna screw off the push an take me time doin' of it.'

Mother Hubbard sighed deeply, and without further speech motioned him to leave the room before her. Tom passed out into the large apartment and, seeing his guide known as Larry the Fly, seated at a vacant table, he crossed and joined him.

'We'll 'ave a cuppler pots,' he said. 'I wants to screw orf this mob.'

'Did you get wot you wanted orf Mother 'Ubbard?'

'No.'

'Wot did she say?'

'Said to get out whiles the gettin' was good. Go on, order a cuppler pots.'

Larry the Fly caught the attention of one of three servers in this up-to-date underworld club. The man brought the beer and gave Larry the Fly a chit. And after glancing at the chit Larry the Fly cringed and looked up into the server's face.

'I ain't done no 'arm,' he whined; 'Wot cher lookin' at me like that for? I ain't done no 'arm.'

26

Poisoned Needle

Old Masters' secretary entered the holy of holies at the top of the great building - and was waved out. Old Masters was engrossed by the reports of the inquest held on the body of a Mr. Harrison, a co-trustee of Mr. Tindale, and of the kidnapping of Senor Alverey.

Harrison, a retired Islands trader, had been standing at the curb of Cathedral Corner when a policeman asked him what was wrong, and Harrison said he had been stung on the back of the neck by a wasp. The next second he was dead.

The wasp's sting was found to be a needle deeply embedded in Harrison's neck, and at the inquest the medical experts stated that on that needle had been smeared a virulent poison which acted like snake venom - the same poison which had killed *Olary Boy* and *Pieface.*

On the night of the inquest, Senor Alverey had had mounted outside his hotel suite a squad of his sailors, under one of his own ship's officers. An alleged American visitor and his valet had, at two o'clock in the morning, drugged the man on duty and then had held up the officer and the remaining men in their room, and had gagged and bound them. When eventually one of these men succeeded in gaining his freedom and releasing his companions, they rushed to the suite occupied by their employer, were obliged to break down the door, and then discovered the Argentinian's valet bound and gagged on the floor of the dressing-room and Alverey vanished.

Alverey's valet told how he had been awakened too late to offer resistance to two men who had gained entry, and then went on to detail the actions of a third man who entered some time after the first two had departed with his master, who was thought to have been drugged. This third man made no attempt to release the valet. He was masked by a blue silk handkerchief. He was in the bedroom when the seamen hammered on the door, but when they finally rushed in the third intruder had vanished through the window.

Old Masters drummed his fingers on the arms of his chair. In the first place, what actuated the kidnapping? Why had Alverey taken all those extraordinary precautions? And what of his instructions to the secretary to purchase leather rigouts and leather hoods, so that he and the valet could be taken, closely guarded, to the ship. Why the leather leggings, overcoats, hoods? Obviously not for a mere disguise: obviously as a measure of defence against something. What was it Alverey had feared?

The secretary silently came in again. On the threshold, he paused to regard Old Masters with astonishment, for his irate employer was sitting well back in his chair, his leonine head set back as far as the bull neck permitted, and on his face a smile.

The secretary coughed.

Old Master's body was jerked upright.

'Well, what is it?' he asked quite affably.

'Mr. Mason of the C. I. B. wishes to see you, sir. I told him you were very busy, but he is insistent.'

'Then why the devil didn't you show him in?'

'Very good, sir,' the secretary replied, wondering which was the most changeable - his employer or the weather. Debonair, smiling, Detective Mason strolled to the great desk.

'I had to see you this afternoon, Mr. Masters, because I have consented to take my girl to the pictures this evening,' he said with simple candour.

'Hug-hum! Couldn't afford to take any young girl to a place of entertainment when I was your age,' Old Masters replied, still affable.

'Well, what can I do for you? Sit down.'

Mason chose the leather chair at the end of the desk.

'We would like to know what your business was with Senor Alverey yesterday evening? May I smoke?'

'Of course. Smoke till you're blue. Senor Alverey is an acquaintance of mine.'

'I know that; but what was the purpose of your call?'

Old Masters regarded his questioner with his chin cupped in his hands. He said:

'I could invent a hundred excuses, but I am not going to invent one. I am not going to tell you why I wished to see Senor Alverey. It's no confounded business of yours, or of your superiors.'

'Permit me to differ on that point. Still, we'll let it drop for the present,' Mason drew thoughtfully at his cigarette, before suddenly beaming on the grim old man, then glaring at him. His next question was quite casually put.

'Do you know a man named Hellburg?'

Old Masters visibly jumped.

'I do,' he replied without hesitation.

'Good! Tell me what you know of him, please.'

'I am going to say nothing about the man.'

Ninety-nine men out of a hundred, observing the light in the old man's eyes, and the outward-thrust under-jaw, would have accepted defeat and have been excused. Not so this smiling young detective, whose hobby was the study of precious stones.

'Very well! We will let that drop for a little while. Another question: Why are you so interested in this matter to the extent of having employed an ex-detective?'

Again Old Masters could have found excuses. Once again he scorned such prevarication.

'Of that, too, I shall tell you nothing. You seem to know quite a lot already.'

'Not as much as I want to know, Mr. Masters. If you are interested, I shall tell you a little of what I do know.'

Old Masters made no encouraging invitation, or even a gesture. Mason lit another cigarette.

'Well - shall I talk or get out?' he asked.

'Please yourself.'

'Good! I'll stay and talk. One little thing I know - I know the poison used to kill your son's horse and the man named Harrison.'

'Yes?'

'Yes,' Mason was only guessing, but he was close to the truth.

'The poison is the distilled liquid of a certain bulb found in Africa,' he explained. 'It is far more powerful than strychnine. One drop is sufficient to kill many adults. The name of the bulb I will not tell you, because I do know it. It is a close Union Government secret.'

'Very naturally,' old Masters said dryly.

'Very, Mr. Masters. Now, in return for that interesting piece of news will you tell me why you called on Senor Alverey last night?'

'Do you want a job?' was old Masters surprising counter question. 'I pay one thousand a year to the head of my shop detective staff, vacant since poor Leader was murdered.'

'I will consider that later. Just now tell me why you called on Senor Alverey last night.'

'I admire your tenacity, Mr. Mason. Doing so, I shall answer your question. I went to him to tell him that I knew he had not gone to Sydney as he gave out when he returned from – I think the underworld term it – smoke.'

'How do you know that?' Mason asked a trifle eagerly.

Old Masters laughed again grimly.

'Have you wondered why Alverey ordered the leather leggings, leather overcoats and the leather hoods?' he asked abruptly.

'I have, and I have reached a reasonable conclusion. He feared being poisoned as was Harrison. A needle, the point of which has been steeped in the African bulb poison is what he feared. Leather might stop such a missile, but to make his chances of escape greater, he intended confusing the needle thrower by dressing his valet and himself in similar rig.'

'You are a man of intelligence, Mr. Mason. How do you think the missile is propelled?'

'Theory - just theory.'

'An explorer friend of mine is inclined to believe that it was propelled through a native blow-pipe. He knows a tribe which uses such a weapon only seven inches in length.'

Mason's brown eyes were small; his mouth was stern.

'Seven inches or seven feet in length. I think the needle

160

found in Harrison's neck was propelled from a much more powerful weapon,' he said.

'How did you arrive at the idea of the poison bulb?' asked Old Masters.

'Oh - the killing of the two horses in the Melbourne Cup and the subsequent inquiry was cabled around the world as news,' Mason began in explanation. 'The South African Police Department cabled the recent discovery there of such a bulb as I have described with the known results of its poisonous juice on animals and on its first discoverers.'

'Hum! So the bulb wasn't just a brain wave of your own?'

'No,' Mason affirmed, laughingly. 'Now I have told you something, tell me a little. Was it correct that you did not suffer any loss from your library when Leader was murdered?'

'Nothing. I can never understand just what the murderer was looking for.'

Mason regarded Old Masters steadily.

'Gee! It's a case!' he said rapidly. 'No wonder that better men than I are bluffed by it. Two men murdered by the common knife and two horses and a man murdered by a poisoned needle. Why, it's damnable. The needle throwing feller can walk along the street, do his worst, and calmly continue on his walk. The victim has no chance whatever.'

'None,' agreed the old man grimly.

'Mr. Masters, tell me what you know of Hellburg.'

Slowly Old Masters shook his massive head.

'The little I know I'm keeping,' he said. 'What I know doesn't concern this matter. What I guess is a little wild, so I am keeping that, too. My advice to you is to proceed cautiously. His killing Leader and that other man proves his ruthlessness.'

A dawning smile broke on Mason's alert face.

'How do you know it was Hellburg behind those two murderers?' he demanded.

Perhaps for the first time in his life Old Masters had made a slip and knew it.

'How do YOU know?' he roared.

SENOR ALVEREY

27

A Piece of Scalp

They had parted, Old Masters and Detective Mason, each having benefited a little by the interview, each knowing that the other knew more than a little and each wondering precisely how much.

After Mason left, Old Masters attended to the business which his secretary was anxious to have completed, and at half-past five, the old man was standing before the lofty windows beyond which was his famous roof garden. He stood with his hands behind his back, bushy white brows contracted, mouth set in an iron grimness.

Abruptly there arose in the outer office an uproar. Old Masters could hear his secretary's voice raised in protest: the deeper growl of men's voices, and one voice high-pitched and determined. Even as Old Masters turned, preparatory to walking to his desk and thumping his heel thereon, the door burst open and there surged into this solemn sanctuary a veritable flood of men.

'Silence! Damn you all – silence!' he roared in tones which drowned the vocal cacophony: 'What is the meaning of all this?'

'I got to 'ave a word with you, Mr. Masters, and these water-drinking owls try to stop me,' gasped Tom Pink, to add to a burly shop detective: 'Let go, you, or I'll chew yer face.'

'Sims - ring for the police,' Old Masters instructed the secretary.

'That's right! Ring for the police, you fool, and spoil everythink. I'm telling you I'm Tom Pink, Mr. Roy's jockey.'

'Sims - you will not ring for the police. You others, get out. Sims - brandy and soda. Good God, man! What have you been doing?'

'No booze, thanks. Bring me a cupper tea,' Tom said unsteadily.

'And a doctor,' added Old Masters.

'Doctor, me foot! Make the cupper tea a pot of tea and plenty of sugar. Say, you are Mr. Roy's father, ain't you?'

Old Masters inclined his head. The spectacle which Tom Pink presented was amazing. His soiled clothes were in rags. His face, neck and bald head were reddened by grime and blood - but his grey eyes were clear and living, and his mouth was stretched by a wide and terrible leer.

'Yes, I am Mr. Masters. You appear to have been in the wars.'

'Too right,' Tom agreed. 'But you ought to see the other bloke. Say - gimme one of them cigars to smoke whiles the tea is coming, will you. I got somethink important to say when I gits me breath.'

'Sit down in that chair and help yourself,' Old Masters invited.

'Thanks,' Tom Pink almost fell into the chair, reached for and took one of the Duplex Havanas, bit off the end - which made Old Masters shiver at the sacrilege - and put one hand into a trousers pocket for a match.

'Cripes, that's funny!' he said. When he withdrew his hand the fingers held a hairy object. This the jockey set down on the spotless desk. Then he chuckled.

'Why, in the 'eat of the moment, like, I musta put a bit of the Scorpion's scalp in me pocket.'

'Indeed! And who is the Scorpion?'

''E was the bloke I 'ad the argument with. 'E's in tow with them one, two, three and four over four fellers.'

'Oh—'

'Oh, yes - I've 'ad a great time, although you wouldn't think it to look at me,' Tom explained, drawing at the cigar, and actually inhaling deeply. 'Thank 'eavens, 'er's the tea.' Then to the secretary when he set the tray on the desk: 'Of course you would bring a thimble for a cup, wouldn't you? Never mind. I'll manage.'

'Shall I not bring bandages, sir?' Sims asked Old Masters. 'Are they knife wounds?'

'Oh - no. That's only scratches from other blokes' fingernails and teeth. But you oughter see 'em. It'd do your sore eyes good.'

'That will be all, Sims,' Old Masters ordered. Then, when the secretary had gone; 'Now, Pink, what have you been doing since you disappeared?'

In his inimitable racy speech, Tom Pink began with his meeting with Larry the Fly, his payment of fifty pounds for information, his borrowing of that amount from Diana Ross, and his arrival in Larry the Fly's company at Old Mother Hubbard's establishment. Then followed a horrific description of an attempt to torture him with scorpions, an attempt which failed when the insects refused to sting his bared chest.

'You see, one night last March I got drunk in Louth, on the river Darling,' he further explained. 'It was a 'ot night and it was beginning to rain. Not that I cared if it snowed. But I fell down asleep against the pub wood 'eap, and that wood 'eap was alive with scorpions and centipedes. The rain brought 'em orl out, and when I woke up about dawn I was covered with 'em.

'I thought they was non-living ants and started to brush 'em off me, and before I knoo what was what I got stung by three scorpions and about seven 'undred centipedes. Cripes! I was in a mess! It was the whisky and the brandy still in me wot saved the situation. All the same, I 'ad to be rushed to 'orspital at Wentworth about a 'undred miles south. An' the quack there told me I was lucky to be alive, and, also, that I would be immune from scorpion stings for about three years.

'An' I am, too. So when the Scorpion dumps 'is breeders -'E breeds 'em to fight bull-ants for the Chows, you know – on me chest they all refused to do their stuff, just like the Wentworth quack said they would.

'The Scorpion – that's a bit of 'im on the desk there – 'E put 'is friends back to their box and goes off for a darning needle to heat in the lamp, and while 'e's gorn, I gets out of the rope I'm trussed with, 'im having loosed it when he wanted to bare me chest.

'Back he comes with the darning needle. I 'ad moved the lamp and the table and the scorpions into the corner so's we'd 'ave a fair go. An' we 'ad it, too. 'E fought well, did the Scorpion. Why, we musta bin at it for about 'alf an hour, but I'm blessed if I remember putting nigh 'alf 'is scalp in me pocket. Funny, ain't it, a bloke don't remember things 'e does when 'e's orl 'otted up.

'Any'ow, to make a long story short, I got 'im trussed on the bed like I 'ad been trussed. To the bed I brought the table with the lamp and the box of scorpions on it. The chair, too. Then I starts 'unting for information.

'Oh, no! The scorpions never actually stung the bloke. You see I chucked a bit of cloth over the Scorpion's face, and when he was obstinate I got out his beautiful Java Queen; pressed on her sting with the end of the darning needle, and then when she was 'anging on to the Scorpion's chest with her nippers, I pricked 'im with the darning needle.

''E didn't want no more persuading when I took off the cloth and let 'im see the Orstralian specimen wriggling over his nose between the forceps.'

'And what did he tell you?' Old Masters asked impatiently, when Tom ceased talking to drink another 'thimble' of tea.

'Why, that he was one of the gang run by a bloke named Hellburg. Hellburg's lootenants go by number, One of Four up to Four of Four. They doped *Olary Boy* at Caulfield and *Pieface* at Wodonga, but they never 'ad nothink to do with killing the 'orses in the Melbourne Cup.

'The Melbourne Cup poisoners knocked 'em rotten. They 'ad a last minute stunt all readied but wasn't able to put it on. It was Alverey 'oo dooked 'em in the first place, and it was Alverey they thinks done the job scientific like when they failed. Four of Four is a qualified quack an' 'e got mad to know 'ow Alverey worked it.

'An' there's more. I got outer the Scorpion the names of them numbered blokes, but 'oo Hellburg is the Scorpion didn't know. 'E knows, however, that the numbered blokes don't know Hellburg either. When they sees Hellburg, orl they sees is a bloke wearin' a white hood over 'is dial.

'Anyway, just when I finishes with the Scorpion, two of

the gang cum in, and there was further argument. I tells 'em I was trying to make the Scorpion tork and couldn't, and the Scorpion backs me up knowing they'd snuff us both if they knoo 'e 'ad told me wot 'e 'ad done.

'I gits shoved into a 'ole for a long time. Must a been days. Orl they gimme was bread and cheese an' water. An' then the Scorpion sneaks in and puts the acid on me to promise 'im two 'undred quid if 'e gets me clear. I thinks of Mr. Cusack and Mr. Roy. I swears blind I'll get 'im the money, trustin' Mr. Cusack and Mr. Roy will back me work.

'Then it comes out that Hellburg 'as given orders that I am not to be snuffed; keeping me fer somethink like the nigs kept the missionary, I suppose. The gang is gettin' windy. They've got Alverey, seems like, but just where I couldn't find out. The Scorpion - 'e's on the make, but 'e's as nervous as a cat, an' with reason.

'I fixed a deal with 'im. Two hundred quid to let me out, and another two 'undred to be paid when 'e parts up with the information when and where to snaffle the bloomin' lot - without 'im, of course.

'I got away late this morning, and I 'ad to 'ide up 'ere and there, and get 'ere in kind of stages, with about a million crooks orl hotted up about me. And then more arguments getting to Mr. Roy's office, to find 'im out, and more arguments still gettin' up 'ere to you.'

'Hug-hum! Four hundred pounds is a lot of money,' Old Masters objected.

'Orl right!' Tom said, standing up. 'I'll get the doin's off Mr. Roy.'

'Sit down, Pink. Of course, I'll find the money.'

28

In Grave Danger

At about eleven o'clock on the Saturday morning, Roy emerged from the Collins Street branch of one of the great banks, where he had been on his own business. And almost the first person he saw among the passing people was Dick Cusack.

'Hullo, Dick, why the gloom?' he asked, laying a restraining hand on his friend's arm.

'I wish tomorrow would come quicker,' Dick said with a wry smile.

'So do I. I wish Diana had told us in the tea-shop the other day which of us she loved and put the other beyond suspense. Do you think she loves you, old man?'

Dick slowed in his walk, and before replying edged them both close to a hatter's window which they came to face without having interest in the stock.

'Sometimes I do, and sometimes I don't,' he said.

'And that is how I feel about it,' Roy admitted. 'Anyway, the lucky one must insist on an early marriage so that he can take her right away from all the mystery and trouble.'

'You bet. And I'll be feeling bad if it is you, and yet glad that it is you. Irish, isn't it?'

'Very. It is the way it's with me, Dick. We've played fair and that's something to our credit. We—'

Standing semi-inclined to each other, their heads but eighteen inches apart, both caught the flash of some silver object as it passed between them. A tinkling note as it struck the plate-glass window was followed by another at their feet. Both looked down - and saw on the pavement the tiny sewing needle.

Simultaneously both swung round to face the crowd. The morning being fresh, they saw the usual bevy of men wearing overcoats and of women in costumes and furs. But not a face which could be recognised.

Dick stooped and carefully retrieved the needle.

The eye-hole was filled with a dull white substance.

'Well - and that's that?' Dick said slowly, and paused for a moment before emptying the contents of his matchbox and placing the needle therein. 'Question is - how many more needles has that swine got on him right now?'

'And another question, Dick. Whom did he aim at?'

'At us, of course.'

'Yes, I know. But which one?'

'Search me. What are we going to do about it?'

'I vote we go along to the old Dad right away.'

'Come on, then.'

'I wonder why they are picking us?' Roy said, as they shot skywards in one of the lifts two minutes later.

'Ask me another. Why did they pick on poor old Harrison?'

On the top floor, when they stepped from the lift, they found four people waiting to descend. Roy walked by them, but Dick raised his hat to a fashionably dressed girl.

'Didn't you recognise her?' Dick asked whilst they walked the corridor to Old Masters's office.

'No. Who?'

'One of Tindale's maids. My word! She was dressed smartly. Wouldn't take her for a maid; although why I should think maids are not smartly dressed, I don't know.'

'Mr. Masters engaged?' Roy asked the much abused Sims.

'Not at the moment, Mr. Roy.'

'Come on in, Dick.'

Old Masters they found walking to and fro across his huge room, his hands clasped behind his broad back.

'Hullo, Dick!' he said, grimly smiling.

'Morning, Mr. Masters,' Dick responded. 'I met Roy coming out of the bank. For a moment or so we stood facing a shop window whilst we talked. And then this needle passed between our heads, struck the window and fell to the pavement.'

Old Masters almost leapt the distance between himself and the matchbox held out in Dick's hand.

'Let me see it!' he commanded sharply.

He took it to the big desk, seated himself there before opening the box. With a reading glass he studied the needle of death. Second after second went by. Unheeded, Roy and Dick seated themselves, to start with quite excusable fear at the sight of the old man now holding the needle against the desk electric with a pair of tweezers.

'Just imagine a devil like that walking around Melbourne,' Dick said quietly. 'I'd - I'd like to get my hands on him!'

'Hum! You have got no idea which one he aimed at?'

Dick shook his head.

'None whatever, Dad,' Roy confessed, marking the significance of the old man's question.

'I wonder—' Old Masters paused to reflect. Then: 'I wonder if he carries more than one prepared needle when he goes on the murder path? I wonder if, having fired his vile bolt, he has to return to his home to prepare another one.'

'Doubtful. He killed two horses in the same five minutes.'

'What beats me is that no one saw him fire at Harrison - not even that street pest who was sitting on the seat beside him. And evidently no one saw anything remarkable in the actions of the swine when he fired at us.'

'You are correct there, Dick. Now, let me think.'

They watched Old Masters, leaning back in his chair, his eyes closed, on his grim face a strange admixture of fatigue, strength and determination. He wanted to think, did Old Masters, and, watching him, his son was tempted to put a dozen questions. Why did Old Masters want to think? Did that brain hold secrets relative to all this criminal activity?

Such a terrifically active brain, too. The litter on the giant desk indicated a hundred and one interests - a small model of an aeroplane, a doll's house complete with furniture, a vase of orchids, an onion – used as a paper weight – resting on a stack of documents. When finally the faded hazel eyes opened, their gaze rested first on Dick Cusack, and then on the face of his son.

'Obviously both you boys are in grave danger,' he said. 'That devil with the blow-pipe, or whatever it is he fires the needle with, will try again. That is certain. I wish I knew which of you he wants out of the way. But that I'll find out shortly. Now we have to evolve methods assuring absolute immunity from a future attack. You both must go to my house and stay there.'

'Why your house, Dad? It would only direct his attention

to you,' Roy pointed out.

'Where else can you go? Why, you must not walk openly in the street! Come - I know what we'll do.'

Favouring Old Masters' plan in lieu of anything better, Roy and Dick accompanied the old man down to the lift and to the ground floor. He then led them to the packing room and the ramp, from which a fleet of vans rushed goods to railway stations and to all the suburbs. Pausing beside one of the enclosed vans, he said:

'This one will do. Get in.'

'Get - whatever for?'

'Get in,' roared Old Masters. 'The thickness of the van's sides will stop a needle.'

'All right! Come on, Dick,' the astonished Roy exclaimed, seeing the urgency of this mode of transport, yet angry and a little humiliated.

Old Masters himself locked the double doors of the van. They heard him gruffly instruct the driver to proceed direct to the house near St. Kilda beach.

They were passing along Swanston Street, when Old Masters was ringing up Mr. Tindale's house. They were crossing over Princes Bridge whilst Old Masters was asking Diana, as a very great favour, to leave at once to call on him.

At the gate to the old man's spacious home, the driver opened the double doors of the van, it was a little comfort that there was no one then in the road to observe them inelegantly getting out. Joyce admitted them at once.

'Mr. Masters has just rung through, sir,' he announced. 'I am to say, sir, that neither of you is to go outside, even into the garden, before he arrives for lunch.'

'Very well, Joyce.'

'Any whisky in the sideboard?' asked Dick.

'Yes, Mr. Cusack.'

'Then I'm having a gargle, Roy,' Dick said earnestly. 'I am badly in need of it.'

'You will find Mr. Pink in the dining room,' Joyce informed them.

'Pink! Tom Pink! Why, has he turned up?'

'Yes, sir.'

Hurriedly, both men dashed for the dining room.

On the floor sitting on a space covered with newspaper, Tom Pink sat diligently working on a hefty mallee root with a carving knife.

29

The Scorpion

The mallee root was not exceptionally big, and, with the carving knife, Tom Pink had removed all the spiked and jagged splinters. At the business end it was no longer than an emu egg, and tapering sharply for two feet it now appeared as one of those schoolboy dreams much enlarged - a toffee-dipped apple stuck on a stick.

'I've got a date tonight, and, as I haven't been able to lay me 'ands on me ole shillelagh, I bin puttin' in time on this root.'

'The carving knife, sir!' exclaimed the scandalised valet-butler-slave.

'Don't worry. I got a file, and I'll sharpen her up when I've done. Meet me friend and enemy, gentlemen - Mr. Ivor Stanhope, otherwise the Scorpion.'

From the man sitting on the spread sheets of newspaper, Tom Pink dressed in new but not exactly well-fitting clothes, the friends gave their attention to the man lounging in a chair by the window. His clothes were passable, but the crown of his head was bandaged, and one arm was in a sling.

'You appear to have been in trouble, Mr. Stanhope,' Roy ventured to this man, whose attention had been given to the narrow space between the drawn blind and the window frame. Offering no explanation, he nodded surlily, and continued to peer through the chink at the drive and the road gate at its end.

'Not exactly trouble, Mr. Roy,' Tom pointed out deprecatorily. 'Me and 'im 'ad a light argument and I accidentally pulled a bit of 'is scalp off. Then 'e fell against a table, awkward like, and broke 'is arm.'

'Is that so?' Dick asked with a grin of amusement. 'And how did you come out of the argument?'

'Me? Oh - I got me face up against 'is fingernails some'ow, but it wasn't 'is fault.'

'No, of course not!' Roy agreed, wanting badly to laugh. 'Now, perhaps, you will tell us where you have been these last few days. Thanks, Joyce. Having a drink, Tom?'

'Not just now, Mr. Roy. It affects me eyesight,' declined Tom, his gaze fixed on his work of carving.

'All right. Tell us what you have been doing.'

'Oh - just been away visiting people I used to know,' the jockey said indifferently.

'During which time you met Mr. Stanhope and entered into an argument?'

'That's so.'

'You're mighty close,' stated Dick. 'When did you come back out of smoke?'

'Cuppler days ago, Mr. Masters arst me to take a rest in 'is 'ouse, which is why you finds me 'ere.'

'Did you get the information you desired?'

'Wot information?'

'You know. Who doped *Olary Boy*?'

'Some of it.'

'Come - come! Why don't you bring it out?'

'Bring out wot, Mr. Roy?'

Roy sighed.

'What shall we do with him, Dick?'

'Shall we jump him round a bit?' suggested Dick Cusack.

'Better leave him alone, mister,' advised Mr. Ivor Stanhope. 'He's a volcano, that's wot he is.'

Try as they would, Roy and Dick could get nothing out of Tom Pink, and were no more successful when they tackled the Scorpion.

A few minutes after twelve o'clock, Old Masters rang up further to impress upon them the urgency of not leaving the house, even to walk in the garden. A friend of his would be calling to stay to lunch, and he himself would be there about one o'clock.

At half-past twelve, Joyce announced a Mr. Wilson.

Mr. Wilson was a large man, redfaced, sporting a grey moustache with fiercely pointed waxed ends. Roy recognised him as one of the shop detectives.

'Why, if it ain't the ole sergeant-major 'oo argued the point with me up orl them flights of stairs when I wanted to 'ave a word with Mr. Masters,' Tom said, springing to his feet: 'You are not wishing to continue the argument, are you?'

'I am not,' Wilson replied emphatically. To add with a sudden broad smile. 'You are the toughest customer I ever had to handle.'

'Attempted to 'andle, you mean.'

'Perhaps you are right.'

'What are you here for, Wilson?' Roy inquired.

'My orders, sir, are to prevent either Mr. Cusack or yourself from leaving the house.'

'You don't mean to infer that you are intending to keep us prisoners, surely?'

177

'Those are my orders, sir,' Wilson admitted with obvious reluctance.

'Whose orders?'

'Old—pardon, sir – Mr. Masters' orders.'

'He must think we are a couple of kids, Dick,' was Roy's half angry supposition. And they settled down to wait.

At nine minutes to one, Joyce announced Miss Leven, and into the room stepped a smartly dressed brunette, the same girl whom Dick had recognised as Tindale's maid when Roy and he stepped out of the lift.

'We are certainly getting a succession of surprises today,' he said, beaming on Miss Leven.

She smiled at them all, saying:

'I have been ordered to take lunch with you.'

At one o'clock precisely, Old Masters arrived.

'Hum! Well, you're all here. Joyce - lunch!'

'I have laid it in the morning room, sir.'

'Why? Why the devil not here?' demanded the old man.

'Well, sir - you see sir! Er - Mr. Pink, sir, has been engaged, sir.'

'Hug-hum! What are you up to, Pink?'

'I bin workin' up a new shillelagh, Mr. Masters,' explained Tom, lurching to his feet and showing the result of his labours.

From the evil-looking club, Old Masters' eyes rose to hold Tom's glance. Very softly he asked:

'Is it heavy.'

'Too right, it's heavy.'

That made Old Masters' face break into a rare smile.

Old Masters entertained an unusual company at lunch, proving himself to be an ideal host. On edge with curiosity,

Roy studied them all in turn; the silent Mr. Ivor Stanhope, who, although his names were suitable for the screen, gave no visual hint of ever being anything other than a villain; the not silent Tom Pink; the demure Miss Leven; and the most polite Mr. Wilson. When lunch was over, Old Masters made known his wishes.

'During the afternoon,' he said. 'I want you people to stay in the dining-room after you have selected any books which may take your fancy and which you will find in the lounge. I am expecting several visitors whom I shall see in the library. Is that clear?'

'It is - and it is not,' Roy argued. 'I would like to know—'

'Roy - you will know nothing,' Old Masters cut in. 'If you or Dick, or Mr. Stanhope, or Miss Leven leaves this house you will almost certainly go out to your deaths.'

'But - but - it's all so extraordinary, Dad.'

'It is - and devilish. I will say no more.'

With a glare in his eyes, and his square jaw thrust forward, Old Masters courteously bowed to Miss Leven and withdrew.

'What are you doing in this galley, Miss Leven? Didn't I see you in Mr. Tindale's house?' asked Roy, curiously.

'I can't answer questions, Mr. Cusack,' she replied.

As requested by their host, these ill-assorted guests took books and magazines to the dining-room; whereupon the Scorpion at once occupied his former station at the window.

'Can't understand what Tindale's maid is doing here,' Dick whispered to his friend.

'Tindale's maid? Who?'

Miss Leven. She waited at table once when I dined with Diana and Tindale.'

'Miss Leven! Tindale's maid! Why she's one of our smartest shop detectives!'

A little after three o'clock, Mr. Ivor Stanhope uttered an oath.

'Wot's up with you?' demanded Tom Pink, sunk in a comfortable chair and busy with the autobiography of a famous jockey.

'The D—'s. There's two of 'em comin' up the drive. Where shall I get?'

'Stay put,' Tom calmly advised 'If you crawls under the table they laugh hard. But they won't be comin' in 'ere.'

Nor, indeed, did Sub-Inspector Dawson or Detective Mason enter the dining room. They were soon closeted with Old Masters in the library, where they remained. Slowly the afternoon dragged away for Roy and Dick. Joyce came in and said Old Masters wished to speak with Tom Pink. And when Tom Pink came back, Miss Leven departed for the same purpose. On her return the Scorpion was called, and reluctantly and with obvious uneasiness, he, too, passed out.

At dinner, in addition to those who sat down at lunch, there were present Detective Mason, Detective-Sergeant Wallis and Sub-Inspector Dawson.

At ten o'clock Old Masters, the three policemen and Tom Pink left the house.

At eleven Miss Leven retired to the room made ready for her.

At nine minutes past twelve, Diana rang up.

'Roy! Is that you, Roy? Yes - yes! Is Dick there, too? He is? Then please come as quickly as possible. Something has happened to guardie. He - he's been murdered.'

'Come on, Dick,' Roy urged. 'Knock out anyone who tries to stop us going to Diana.'

30

The Hooded Man

Seated round a table in the back room of a secluded house not far from Coburg railway station were four men. He at the head of the table was effectively disguised by the white hood enveloping his head. On this man's left sat Three of Four, a silver-haired man always smiling. Opposite him sat One of Four, whilst opposite Hellburg – the hooded man – lounged Mr. Josman, who had engineered the second kidnapping of Senor Alverey, and whose designation was Four of Four.

These men, with another who guarded the front door, and two others who were with Alverey in the front room, had all arrived after midnight at this unlet furnished house.

'Is Alverey here?' asked Hellburg at length in peculiarly soft tones, a mere trace of a foreign accent in his voice.

'Yes, Hellburg,' replied Mr. Josman. 'Have him in?'

Hellburg nodded and fell to looking at a brown paper parcel. He motioned to One of Four to remove Josman's tray. Josman re-entered and seated himself between One of Four and Hellburg leaving the bottom end of the table vacant for the two men who came in with Alverey to stand before them.

'You were successful?' Hellburg asked Four of Four.

'Quite,' was the reply.

'Now, Senor, the moment has arrived for you to decide

whether to return to your own country or remain in Australia - dead,' the suave, gentle voice said. 'Your information has proved correct, and, so far as I am concerned, there is no need for your captivity to be prolonged.'

'I may take a chair?' Alverey asked coldly.

'Pardon! By all means.'

'Good. Now speak on.'

'My decision concerning you is not dictated by humanity, dear Senor Alverey. I am concerned only with the fact that to us you are more valuable alive than dead. Consequently I am prepared to permit you to board your yacht and steam away to South America when you have paid to us the sum of twenty thousand pounds. Can you raise twenty thousand pounds on Monday, Tuesday?'

'Yes, you brigand,' Alverey answered with courage. 'I shall pay the money on Monday afternoon.'

'Very well. Now listen carefully.' The Argentinian was instructed how, when, and where he was to hand over the money.

'What I wish to impress on you is this,' Hellburg proceeded. 'Any double crossing on your part will inevitably result in your death from a poison needle. Should eventually I discover that any effort has been made to mark, note the numbers, or otherwise seek to trace the money. I shall follow you to South America and there deliver the needle. Being a man of intelligence, and of imagination, you will easily understand - er - your mental condition when expecting, but never knowing the instant you will feel the sting of that poisoned needle. In fact, I believe you will agree with me that double crossing is rigidly to be avoided.'

'How am I to know you will not follow to South America

and with the threat of the needle there – what you say? – menace me?'

'Yes, there is that, I admit,' purred Hellburg. 'We will not, however, discuss a supposition. You will arrange the more pressing matter of the twenty thousand on Monday afternoon?'

Alverey nodded.

'Good! I want you to accept my apologies for having put you to so much inconvenience. It was, after all, the result of extraordinary circumstances. You will admit that after having instructed us to prevent two horses from reaching Melbourne Cup form, after having upbraided us for not doing the work thoroughly, and eventually failing to carry out our pre-Cup plan through the default of a trusted member, we were, no less than the public astounded to see those identical horses drop dead.

'Obviously it was necessary for us to discover our more successful rival, and most especially the method he adopted. We are always keen to consider new ideas.

'Naturally, we thought you were that rival, and, therefore, had to question you. Your own obstinacy only stood in the way of your freedom. What you eventually told us about the John Ross Trust, allied with the killing of one of the trustees, put us on to the poisoners who evolved so splendid a weapon able to project such a unique poison.

'Well, Senor Alverey, goodbye. It will not be, I sincerely hope, merely au revoir. In about half an hour you will be conveyed from this place and permitted to step from the car which brought you here - a free man. That will be all.'

Maintaining silence, Alverey rose. He regarded each of the lieutenants steadily, smiled grimly at the hooded chief, and walked out with his gaolers. After all, what was there for him to say.

Four of Four took his place at the bottom end of the table.

'Now, Four of Four, what have you to show us?' Hellburg asked.

'In that package are six of the bulbs from which the poison was distilled.'

Hellburg untied the string and folded back the paper from the several bulbs which appeared similar to old onions.'

'Well, one would not think that such small globes contained so powerful a poison,' Hellburg murmured. 'Did you find any formula?'

'Several. Here they are. They cover the whole process from distilling the poison to fixing it in semi-soluble form.'

The documents were handed to Hellburg, who did not examine them.

'What else? The blow pipe?' he asked.

'No. This,' and Four of Four held in his hand a peculiarly shaped pistol. 'It is a powerful airgun,' he explained. 'You break it, so. Here you see is a disc of cork. The needle is gently fixed into the cork and then the needle is slipped into the breech, the cork entering last. The air is compressed by the closing of the breech, and when the gun is fixed the cork is caught at the end of the barrel, the needle continuing on, the eye-hole end, which contains the poison, travelling first and assisting the missile in keeping straight.'

'Very interesting. Pass me the weapon, please.'

But Four of Four drew back with a grim smile.

'I have been thinking of keeping it,' he said. 'As a matter of fact, Hellburg, I can run this crowd better than you. There is that little matter concerning the last divi. I don't forget anything. I'm going to give you a taste of the needle in this gun now - and after this I'll run this show.'

So saying, Four of Four rose to his feet, towering above the seated three, as he pointed the dreadful pistol at Hellburg's face. The latter's expression altered not one whit.

'This - is rather sudden,' he said, almost with a giggle.

'It is, Hellburg. You know too much about us. You know I killed Leader, and you know Matthews killed the other man in mistake for Leader. You have got too much on us, and we've got absolutely nothing on you. We have never even seen your face. Now we don't want you. We'll be better off without you.'

Followed a moment's tense silence. Then the man who continually smiled drawled:

'You can count me out of this Josman. I've got you covered. If you fire that thing at Hellburg, you'll make a second dead man here. Cut it out.'

For a second, two seconds, Four of Four hesitated; then he broke into uneasy laughter and sat down.

'I was only joking,' he explained, as he slid the air pistol across the table to Hellburg. 'We'll have to have others made in the same pattern. Why, with a pistol like that you could get away with anything. You could rule the city.'

'You will never do any ruling, Four of Four. I don't like your jokes,' Hellburg said softly.

He pressed the trigger of the gun, and there flashed between the others a needle, to stop, half buried, in Josman's left eye.

31

The Aftermath

Four of Four's hand flashed to the wound. For the moment he was completely blind and frantically he searched for a handkerchief.

Three of Four and One of Four looked at him with wolfish interest. In Hellburg's right hand an automatic pistol was aimed at the doomed man.

'You dirty swine, Hellburg! Oh, you dirty swine! Oh, why didn't I fire the thing at you? But I'll live long enough—'

A groping hand sought frantically for his gun, whilst sobs of terror and of anguish escaped his lips. Yet even as his fingers closed over the pistol butt in his pocket he died.

'Well, they will never hang Tindale's murderer,' said Hellburg steadily, his voice in no way altered from its accustomed softness and smoothness, as he glanced grimly at the rest.

'Did he kill Tindale?' asked One of Four.

'So Two of Four told me when I came in. I told the fool to avoid killing. I will not have unnecessary killings, as I have often told you. It arouses the police to frenzy. And Four of Four needn't have killed Tindale. If he hadn't we might have got a second twenty thousand from him.'

'What are you going—?'

From the passage came a dull smack which preceded a duller thud.

'One,' exclaimed a man's voice, in the passage.

'See what's the matter out there, Three of Four,' Hellburg rapped out, sharply swinging round.

The latter nodded obedience, and strode to the door, which was wide open. The remaining two watched him in tense silence, as he paused before the door frame, and then began cautiously to move around the left hand post, his ready automatic held before him. Then the seated men both saw the mallee root strike Three of Four full on the temple - and he pitched heavily to the carpet of the passage.

'Two,' came Pink's voice, to be followed by a curt command, which sent Hellburg leaping to his feet.

'Now then, Hellburg, and you other men! You had better surrender,' came the voice of Sub-Inspector Dawson. 'You are cut off. The house is completely surrounded.'

With a quick, despairing glance round, One of Four crept across the room, gained position behind the door and slammed it. A mighty blow from Tom's shillelagh smashed the lock and sent the door wide once more as Hellburg fired at the electric light, hit it and plunged the room into darkness. Then a beam of wood smashed against the window, smashed again and again till barely the frame was left. An invisible hand tore down the blind and curtains. From the outer darkness, brilliant motor headlamps flashed out, their beams directed through the wrecked window, illuminating the room.

'Better give in, Hellburg,' Dawson advised again from the passage.

'I never give in,' Hellburg shouted, to add with faint Irish brogue, 'Good-bye, Tommy! After all I should have had your throat cut.'

A pistol shot rang out - to be followed by silence for a few seconds. Then the man known as One of Four spoke. 'I give in,' he declared. 'See - I'm chuckin' me gun out through the window.'

'March out through that door, hands above your head,' ordered Dawson.

And so they took Three of Four. He was still smiling. Police poured into the room through door and window, with them Tom Pink and Senor Alverey, whose guards had a minute before been held at gun point by one of many policemen who had been in the house long before the gang and the prisoner had arrived. The two stunned men in the passage were hastily handcuffed. The greatest shock was yet to come.

'Cripes!' exclaimed Tom Pink incredulously when he came to stare down into the painted face of Mother Hubbard, from whose head the white hood had been taken.

'So you see, when Alverey set Hellburg on to dope *Olary Boy* and *Pieface* to make sure neither of his rivals would win the Cup, he stirred up a hornet's nest,' Old Masters was saying a few days later when faced by Diana, then his guest, his son and Dick Cusack.

'The trouble with Tindale started when he learned from the babbling Mr. Harrison that Alverey knew of Diana's father's secret wishes. By his will, you remember, he left his estate in sole control of Tindale and Harrison, after having verbally told them that from the trust they each were to receive two thousand a year for life. The bulk of the fortune was to be handed to you, Diana, the day following your wedding or when you reached the age of thirty five. To save you from fortune hunters, you and the public were not to know that.

'Even with such princely remuneration, Tindale could not go straight. He appropriated thousands and thousands which he wasted on stock exchange and racecourse, safe from prosecution because the money was under his full control, and yet with the secret gun unable not to kill once he killed those racehorses of yours.

'As a check, and a poor one, too, old Mr. Ross wrote down his verbal directions to Tindale and Harrison in a document he left with a firm of lawyers, to be opened by them when Diana married or reached the age of thirty five.

'Although Tindale did not fear criminal prosecution, he feared social ostracism which would have met him when Diana married. He knew Harrison to be, despite his faults, an upright man who, when he learned the financial situation, would make it public.

'Some little thing must have aroused Harrison's suspicions, and, doubtless, he allowed Tindale to know of them. Some time ago Tindale got to know of a poison bulb growing on the shores of Lake Frome which contains a new and deadly poison. A similar bulb has recently been found in South Africa, and so deadly is the poison that its discovery and manufacture have been kept secret by the Union Government. His poisonous needles he fired at the two horses when they were passing along to the racecourse. On account of their size, the poison did not act so quickly as it did with Harrison and late with the member of the gang who murdered Tindale.

'There are many points, of course, which never will be cleared up. Alverey guessed it was Tindale who killed the horses. He was positively sure it was Tindale who killed Harrison, which was why he had the guards mounted. When Hellburg's gang kidnapped him he at first thought it was Tindale who had gained access to his bedroom, and felt even relief when knowing it was not. We can but assume it was Tindale whom the valet saw enter the suite a little after his master had been taken from it, and finally escaped by dropping from the window.

'I first suspected Tindale when Leader discovered how he was secretly plunging on the stock exchange. As we now know, Leader was killed because he discovered Hellburg's identity. I could not associate the killing of your horses with Hellburg's somewhat crude attempts and eventually I got my best woman shop detective into Tindale's house as a maid recently arrived from New Zealand. She brought me one of his bulbs and copies of his formulas, and even then I did not visualise an air pistol which he used so accurately from his raincoat pocket, the lips of which were stiffened with whalebone to keep them open.

'And when Diana confessed to him which of you she loved and determined to marry, again that illogical murder lust, controlled him, and directed the attack on you whilst you stood talking in front of the shop window.

'That, I think, is about—'

The door was flung open and Tom Pink burst into the room.

'I got a 'orse! I cum inter a fortune!' he almost screamed. 'Wot jew think? Ole Alverey 'as given me a bank account of five thousand quid, and - and - oh, wot jew think? He's given me *King's Lee!* Says I can try for the Melbourne Cup next year. An he'll win it, too. I'll knock the greenness outer 'im. I'll stop 'im lookin' at the scenery.'

'Well - that's great, Tom,' Old Masters said beamingly. On his feet he took the jockey's arm, saying, 'Come along to the library and tell me all about it. What have you done with your friend - enemy?'

'The Scorpion? Oh - me and Alverey 'as planted 'im on the yacht. He'll be able to join up with another crook gang in South America.'

'Well - well. We cannot be too rough on him for the belated service he has rendered to society. We'll see you people later.'

'Now, Diana, tell us which,' Roy implored when they three were standing, tensely, drawn taut by emotion. Roy's face was a little white. His eyes were wide and burning. Dick's face, too, was paled, but he stood a little behind his friend.

They watched Diana's lips when they began suddenly to tremble. They saw her eyes cloud, brighten with tears, which presently began to fall.

'Roy - oh, Roy - I am so sorry. I - I - I!'

'It's all right, Diana,' he said with effort. 'It's quite all right. You know I think I guessed it.' Swiftly he turned to Dick, his hand flashing towards his friend. 'I am glad, Dick. Don't forget - I am to be your best man. We played fair, didn't we?'

Dick was unable to speak. He watched Roy leave the room, a stone man. He heard Diana softly crying. And then, when he took her in his arms, he whispered:

'Are - are you sure it's me you love, Diana?'

And Diana nodded her head.

◆

Glossary

bird	a crook, criminal
bob	a shilling
boxing on	to carry on
chit	a letter, or note of authorisation
Chow	a Chinese person
clay	to have sticking power, or determination to finish
Coolgardie stretcher	a canvas camp bed, slung between two poles
corpsed	to murder
crook	something that is bad, not right about the situation
crook's lay	a lair or hiding place
dial	someone's face
divi	the division of cash, or reward
felt	a felt hat, often an Akubra
gargle	an alcoholic drink
gasper	a cigarette
gee gaw	a prize
getting windy	to be nervous
guardie	a personal affectation of 'guardian'
guggle-guggle	a bottle of beer; imitating sounds
hug-hum	clearing the throat; imitating sounds
in smoke	to go into hiding
Irish	to be stupid
John Barleycorn	any malt liquor
know me onions	to know one's head, or limitations
moke	a horse

Molly Macquires	an Irish secret society c. 1848, which dealt in intimidation
mum's the word	to stay quiet, not to say a word
oiler	an oil skin coat
pinching	to arrest a person
q.t.	to be quiet, usually about a secret
runner	a drug dealer
screw off	to take advantage of, to destroy
shillelagh	a wooden club
snow	cocaine
snuffed	to be killed
snuffling a man	to murder a man
sool	to call for someone
spliced	to be married
taken for a ride	to take a person in a car to a convenient place, and then shoot them
tart	an endearing description of a sweetheart, or loved woman
the push	a gang of criminals or convicts
tiff	a fight between lovers
to give the oil	to relate the news, or information
top-notcher	a first class horse
to put the acid on	to make a demand that will either yield results or eliminate the possibility
zac	six pence